D0541665

12597083

From the Chicken House

When I was a boy I always wanted to be on the side of the rebels – Bonnie Prince Charlie, Robin Hood – hiding up trees and fighting back! But what if, suddenly, Britain was invaded and it was all horribly real? Would you be a rebel then? Training to be a spy hero, with guns, codes and disguises, might sound cool – but what if you lost?

Although our nation never had to make that choice, we came very close to losing the Second World War – and this is the story of what could have happened then. It's exciting, stirring and dangerous stuff. In David Tinkler's alternative history you'll discover a very young Queen Elizabeth in exile, a nation overrun by a Nazi invasion, and a bunch of the most unlikely heroes ever!

Come on – let's all join the Resistance and find out what we're made of!

Barry Cunningham
Publisher

NEVER SAY DIE

DAVID TINKLER

Chicken House

2 PALMER STREET, FROME, SOMERSET BA11 1DS

Text © David Tinkler 2014

First published in Great Britain in 2014
The Chicken House
2 Palmer Street
Frome, Somerset, BA11 1DS
United Kingdom
www.doublecluck.com

Cover and interior design by Steve Wells
Typeset by Dorchester Typesetting Group Ltd
Printed and bound in Great Britain by CPI Group (UK) Ltd, Croydon, CR0 4YY

The paper used in this Chicken House book is made from wood grown in sustainable
forests.

1 3 5 7 9 10 8 6 4 2

British Library Cataloguing in Publication data available.

PB ISBN 978-1-908435-37-8
eISBN 978-1-909489-86-8

For Raffie

What if Britain had lost the Second World War?

Well, we nearly did.
And this is the story of what might have
happened next . . .

Keep calm – and never say die!

1

HONEYSUCKLE FARM, DEVON, ENGLAND, 1942

They'd shot his dad, then they'd come for his mother.

Whenever Flint thought about it he cried. He was crying now, but blinking back the tears, and this was because Alfie had said, 'They hang intellectuals and they shoot Resistance.'

A hot tear ran down Flint's nose. He turned his head and pretended to look at the clock – the one that said ten past six. It had said ten past six since ten past six on 13 October 1940, when a Nazi shell had landed on the chicken shed.

Remembering his parents always made the tears come,

yet Flint longed for the past. He dreamt of his old home – Hornbeams, Willow Way, in the county of Surrey. He wanted his dad at the piano singing comic songs. He wanted a hug from his mum and a slice of her lemon drizzle cake.

'Do you know,' Alfie went on cheerfully, 'what an intellectual is?'

Flint shook his head.

Alfie popped a chunk of fried bread into his mouth. 'An intellectual,' he explained with his mouth full, 'is a cross between an egghead and a smart-arse. You'd have most probably grown into one if we'd won the war – only you'd have been a cross between an egghead and a pillock.'

Flint smiled; the tears stopped. Alfie's teasing was always funny, never spiteful. It made him feel as if he had a big brother.

'The bloke that drives the milk lorry says the king's been shot!' announced Alfie.

Flint's eyebrows arched in shock.

'The Gestapo shot him and burnt the corpse. Then they chucked the ashes down a sewer. They had to burn him,' explained Alfie with a grin, 'they couldn't just bury him in case the Resistance dug him up and had him stuffed.'

'What did they shoot him for?' asked Flint anxiously.

'Because he wouldn't kiss Hitler's arse – but his brother will. He thinks the sun shines out of it. So they've made *him* king instead.'

'You mean we've got a traitor king?'

'Until he meets with an accident! That might be a job

2

for you, Flinty – royal assassin!'

'Me?'

'Your dad was a hero – he nearly shot Hitler, didn't he? And Flint is a pirate name. You want to live up to it – be more like a buccaneer and less like a startled canary.'

Good advice – but no one was less like a buccaneer than Benedict Dingle Flint. Pirates don't daydream. They don't saunter about doing the Charlie Chaplin walk or squawk like Daffy Duck. Besides, pirates don't read books, and Flint had a library of three which he read over and over again: *Right Ho, Jeeves, Biggles Flies North,* and *William's Happy Days.* They were all he had left from his former life, apart from his snake belt and a bag of marbles.

The two boys slept in an abandoned Type 28 British anti-tank pillbox at Honeysuckle Farm. Ma Kent, the farmer's wife, woke them every morning just before she fed what was left of the chickens. She gave them their breakfast in the back kitchen as soon as they'd finished milking. It was always fried bread and bacon rind. Old Kent breakfasted on bacon and eggs, even though he was supposed to supply the German Army of Occupation with all the farm's eggs. He ate next door in the snug main kitchen, where the kettle sang and the clock worked.

There was a belch and the sound of boots on flag-stones: Old Kent had finished his breakfast and risen from the table. Even Alfie went silent as the farmer appeared in the doorway. From the nails in his boots to the stubble on his chin he looked like Mr Field the Farmer in Happy Families. But his head had been roasted; the same shell that had blown up the chicken shed had burnt and blinded Old Kent. His mouth opened in the wreck of his face, revealing a perfect set of dentures.

'Are you there?' he asked.

'Yes, sir,' replied Alfie smartly.

'Both of you?'

'Yes,' said Flint.

'Look out the window, Alfie. What do you see?'

'Blue sky, white clouds, and a fresh breeze off the sea.'

'Will it rain?'

'No.'

'Flinty, hitch up Turpin and shift that muck heap – spread it on Three Corner. Alfie, we'll plough Green Meadow.'

'With the tractor?' asked Alfie hopefully. There was a tractor – a grey pre-war Ferguson – which the farmer had taught Alfie to drive by perching himself on a mudguard and barking instructions into the boy's ear. But Green Meadow had not been ploughed since before the invasion. The German 6th Army had landed in the west of England and fought its way through the countryside from hedge to hedge. On their way they'd stormed through Honeysuckle Farm, so lots of nasty stuff – unexploded shells, mines and grenades – could be waiting for them under the grass.

'Safer to use horses,' announced Old Kent. 'They'll set off a mine well ahead of us.'

Alfie didn't argue – the boys didn't argue with Old Kent

– instead, he rolled his eyes and tapped the side of his head. 'Mad!' he mouthed silently to Flint. 'Crazy!' he mouthed to Jock the Border Collie, who'd trotted up to the boys' table, wagging his tail hopefully.

Ma Kent poked her cross-eyes round the door and wagged a finger in Alfie's direction. She thought her husband was mad too – there'd been cows roaming all over that field and none of them had ever been blown up – but Ma Kent didn't approve of cheek. 'It's not safer with horses – that's daft,' she muttered, 'double daft! It won't be a horse that sets one off, it'd be the plough – with you hanging onto it!'

Old Kent considered this advice for several long seconds. 'Right, then,' he said decisively. 'We'll take the tractor.'

Before the war Old Kent had worked the farm with his son Brian, but the battles had been lost, Brian was dead, and all able-bodied men in England between the ages of seventeen and forty-five had been shipped to Germany as slave labour – at least the ones they could catch. Now Old Kent had to run the farm with two boys. He tapped with his stick and led the pair of them into the yard, where Alfie went to start the tractor and Flint disappeared into the richly scented gloom of the cowshed.

Jock the Border Collie had to choose between following the tractor or going with Flint. He was Old Kent's dog, so he should really have gone with his master, but he adored Flint. He loved the way the boy smelt so pleasantly of dung, and Flint never flew into rages; he never kicked out or swore or even shouted. Besides, Flint would often use him as a pillow at night in the pillbox, where there were no beds, just mattresses on the concrete floor. Jock would curl up at the end of Flint's pile of rugs and the boy would nestle his head against him. Then Jock would gently lick his ears.

The collie watched as Flint swept and shovelled. The boy was sluicing a rich mixture of dung and straw down the gutter so that it shot down a hole and out onto the muck pile. The dog sniffed, wagged his tail, and followed Flint out of the cowshed to the stables. Turpin was Flint's favourite carthorse; he was huge, calm and friendly. Jock watched as the big fellow was harnessed and hitched to a cart before being led round to the muck pile.

'I wasn't born to shovel dung,' Flint informed Jock as he forked muck into the cart. The dog pricked up his ears and Turpin turned his head. They loved listening to Flint; they might not have understood, but they knew he was talking to them. 'I was born to be a fighter pilot,' the boy informed them with a modest smile.

In real life Flint might have looked slightly bewildered, but in his dreams he was cool, sharp, and very much like the legendary fighter ace Biggles in *Biggles Flies East*, *Biggles Flies West*, *Biggles Flies North*, and, of course, *Biggles Flies Undone!* (That was one of Alfie's jokes.) There were no muck heaps in Flint's dreams; in his imagination he went about in a flying jacket muttering, 'Great Scott! What the deuce is all this?' and letting fly with his Webley service revolver. Here's the dream he was dreaming as he flung dung into Turpin's cart:

The boys of Greyfriars School listened eagerly as their headmaster introduced the visitor. 'This is Squadron Leader James Bigglesworth, DSO, DFC, MC,' he told them. 'He is here on a mission of grave importance.'

Young Benedict Dingle Flint – known as Firebrand Flint to his many friends – leaned forward alertly. He was only twelve years old, but already a legend at the ancient school because of his lightning reflexes, amazing strength and cool daring.

It was at this point in the dream that Turpin farted. Flint arched his eyebrows in mock horror, but continued to heave muck into the cart. 'Lightning reflexes,' he reminded the horse. 'Amazing strength,' he added. 'Cool daring!' he told Jock.

The richly scented cart steamed gently in the spring sunshine as it lumbered downhill towards Three Corner Field, which faced the sea. Flint lolled comfortably on the seat with the reins in his hands and the sun on his face. He could see the blue Atlantic and hear the distant roll of waves on pebbles, while, in his dream, he'd jumped ahead to where Z Squadron, RAF, was establishing its secret base: *'This is dangerous work,' growled Biggles grimly. 'Under normal circumstances I'd never ask a boy of your age to volunteer for a suicidal mission such as this – but these are not normal circumstances – not by a very long chalk!'*

By the time they reached Three Corner, and Flint had hopped off the cart to open the gate, Biggles was saying, *'Good work, laddie,'* and patting him on the back.

In the old days you spread dung with a pitchfork; you'd

drop piles of muck round the field, then you'd get down and fork it about. That's what Flint started to do, and it was why he didn't see the girl in the dark-blue swing trousers jump the ditch. But she saw him. In fact, she changed direction and ran straight towards him.

'Burn it!' she hissed.

Flint looked up to see a pale face under blonde curls, blue eyes wide in terror. She thrust an exercise book into his hands, turned and bolted for the beach. Flint gaped after her.

A sudden yell came from the other side of the field; a shot rang out as the girl reached the opposite hedge. Flint watched, frozen in horror, as she stumbled. *She must be Resistance!* he guessed. The young woman regained her footing and disappeared down the twisting path that led to the hidden cove. There were more shouts – and now German soldiers in their distinctive jerry helmets were streaming across the field.

But this was no dream; it was war.

Flint glanced at the book that had been thrust into his hand. Slowly it dawned on him that he was holding something very dangerous – something that could get him put up against a wall and shot.

2

'I heard shooting!' yelled Alfie. 'What happened?'

Hens were clucking, pigs were grunting, but Flint was shocked and trembling. He'd unhitched and unharnessed Turpin and was standing next to him as the horse drank from the trough by the stables.

'Nazis,' he explained. 'They were chasing a woman!'

'A woman?'

'Yes,' replied Flint. He remembered her frightened eyes – her curls . . . her tumble of blonde curls. 'Sort of young but grown-up. She was terrified,' he added, and immediately thought that was a really stupid thing to say. Of course she'd have been terrified.

'And they shot her?'

'They shot at her,' replied Flint, 'and she fell – but she might just have tripped, because she kept on running. She gave me a little book.'

'What sort of book?'

'An exercise book – she said I was to burn it – what do you make of that?'

'It's most probably a list of secret codes,' guessed Alfie. 'She didn't want it found on her body.'

'You think she's dead?'

'Probably – where's her book?'

'I buried it under a pile of dung.'

'Good thinking, Flinty,' Alfie nodded. 'We'll go fishing off Flat Rock tonight,' he suggested with the air of a boy who always knew what to do. 'And on the way we'll walk through Three Corner Field and dig it out – then we can burn it, like she said.'

That evening they took their fishing gear and walked through a steep field full of thistles and into Three Corner. It took Flint twenty minutes of poking about with a stick before he found where he'd buried the exercise book. It was stinking, but Alfie grabbed it firmly and led the way down the steep, twisted path to Honeysuckle Cove. Jock followed, wagging his tail. He liked it when they went night fishing – there were always plenty of guts and heads to eat.

The boys lit a driftwood fire up on Flat Rock, the fat, flat wedge of stone jutting out into deep water. They always fished from there, using lugworms or limpets for bait. As soon as the blaze was crackling and the sparks flying up into the smoke, Alfie tore up the exercise book, and page by page Flint fed it to the flames.

'It does look like a list of codes,' muttered Alfie. 'Don't look at them. The less you know, the less you can tell them.'

'I wouldn't tell them anything!'

'Yes, you would. They don't ask nicely.'

The book was ripped up and burnt – even the cover, which just had times tables printed on the back. When there was nothing left of it but ashes Alfie added more driftwood to the blaze. If a Nazi patrol came to investigate, all they'd find would be a cheerful fire and two boys night fishing.

'If any Huns come sniffing round,' said Alfie, 'act dumb.' He was grinning in the firelight; Flint got the impression he'd quite like to have Huns sniffing round, just for the excitement.

'What do you mean – act dumb?'

'Grin at them like the village idiot,' explained Alfie as he baited a hook. 'Give them the impression you're a brick short of a load. Got the idea?'

Flint nodded.

'And don't wet yourself!'

'No,' said Flint. 'Thanks for the advice – I'm sure it's kindly meant.'

'You bet it is,' replied Alfie. He dropped his line into the dark sea. 'I don't want to see you shot, Flinty – a boy of your talents who can squawk like Daffy Duck and burp at will. That would be a sad loss.'

Flint burped by way of reply and bowed modestly in the firelight. 'It's a gift!' he said.

The blazing fire lit up Flat Rock. They usually caught wrasse from the deep water there. But tonight they were lucky; the sea beneath them began to ripple and sparkle and suddenly they were pulling mackerel out of it. The boys gutted a couple of fish and laid them in the embers. Jock sniffed at the flapping pile that were not cooking, turned his head and growled. Flint glanced towards the dark cove. A fierce pinprick of red like a dragon's eye was watching them.

There was a scrunch of feet on pebbles. The tiny red eye dipped down, and a voice called out of the dark, 'Smells good!'

'Who goes there?' cried Alfie. He'd read lots of comics. He knew what to say.

Flint gazed into the dark as a figure scrambled up the rock and approached their fire. The glowing eye turned out to be a cigarette. The man raised it to his lips and took another puff. He was near enough for Flint and Alfie to see the smoke he exhaled in twin jets from his nose – near enough for them to see he had a submachine gun slung across his back. A pair of piercing blue eyes peered at Flint from under a forage cap. The stranger must have been hungry because he stooped down and helped himself to a cooked fish, and then stepped back into the gloom.

'Hullo Alfie,' he said, 'long time no see – how are

things at Honeysuckle Farm? How's poor old Kent?'

'He does his best,' answered Alfie. 'How are things with the Resistance?'

'Never a dull moment! How old are you now, Alfie?'

'Fourteen.'

'Old enough for action – old enough to whet a bayonet. Would you like that?'

'You bet!' cried Alfie. He grinned at Flint, punched the air and darted round the fire so he could watch the heroic figure chewing on a mouthful of fish.

The mysterious bandit looked down at his excited face, swallowed, and asked him, 'Did a young lady pass by in a hurry this morning?'

'Yes,' confirmed Alfie. 'Flint saw her. That's Flint over there.'

'Is he dumb?'

'No,' answered Flint nervously. 'I can talk.'

'Tell me what happened.'

And that's what Flint did. He told him how the girl had run for the corner of the field and how the soldiers had shot at her. 'She dodged down the path, though, and the Germans chased after her. I heard more shots. They must have killed her.'

'They didn't bring back a body,' said the Resistance man.

'You mean she escaped?'

'It's more likely she jumped into the sea off this rock and took her suicide capsule. In which case the fish we're eating will have been eating her, but thanks for the information, lads.' The bandit began to slink back into the darkness. 'You never saw me,' he said, 'because I don't exist.'

There was the sound of feet crunching on pebbles, and then silence.

The boys exchanged glances. Jock whined.

'That was Aka,' whispered Alfie. 'Also Known As!'

'Also known as what?'

'That's his name – Also-Known-As – Aka for short. You heard what he said, Flinty, I'm old enough to be a bandit! They're going to recruit me!' Alfie danced around the fire. He aimed an imaginary submachine gun at an imaginary Nazi. He drew an imaginary fighting knife from his belt and cut an imaginary throat.

'I'd rather you stayed on the farm,' sighed Flint.

But Alfie was not listening. He was hurling imaginary grenades.

Back in the Type 28 British anti-tank pillbox Alfie prac-tised imaginary garrotting, imaginary strangling and imaginary decapitation with an imaginary chainsaw. 'Old enough to join the Resistance!' he kept saying. *Old enough to fill a shallow grave,* thought Flint. He pulled his rugs over his ears, nestled his head against Jock the Border Collie, closed his eyes, and began to dream.

Firebrand Flint VC, at twelve years old the youngest pilot on the Western Front and already a legend in the Royal Flying Corps, was known throughout the service for his addiction to condensed milk. Indeed, it had been by dropping a tin of the stuff onto the head of Baron Manfred von Richthofen at 3000 feet that the heroic boy had snatched victory from the jaws of certain defeat.

Suddenly Alfie shook his shoulder. 'Listen!' he hissed.

'What?' asked Flint irritably – he'd been having a good time in his dream world, where the bullets always whizzed harmlessly over his head.

'Visitors!' cried Alfie, bounding to the sheet of canvas that acted as their door and pulling it back. Headlights swept down the track towards the ruined farmhouse. A vehicle pulled up, its headlights went out, and car doors slammed in the dark.

'Gestapo!' muttered Alfie. 'What do they want?'

The Gestapo – *Geheime Staatspolizei* – were the Nazi secret police. They were masters of terror and experts in torture, but everything about Vogler looked kindly. His eyes twinkled. His walrus moustache looked as if it had been fed on milk. When Ma Kent opened the door to his polite tap she was reminded of the good-natured old boy who'd carved Pinocchio in the Disney film. She imagined him at home in the Black Forest, surrounded by cuckoo clocks.

'Mrs Kent?' he beamed affably. She nodded. 'May we come in?'

Vogler was wearing a leather coat, as you'd expect from the Gestapo. But the hat that he politely removed as he entered the kitchen was not the usual Gestapo trilby. It was a Tyrolean Alpine hat with a feather. He greeted Old Kent with a friendly smile and held out his hand. The

15

farmer remained seated with his head on one side, listening.

'He can't see you,' explained Ma Kent. 'It's not him being rude.'

'No, no,' Vogler hastened to reassure her. 'It was me being foolish. Allow me to introduce myself: I'm . . .'

'You're a Yank!' Old Kent blurted.

'Not really,' explained Vogler, 'although I was born in Pennsylvania. My family returned to Germany in 1920 when I was eleven. I'm bilingual – English and German – which is useful in these troubled times.'

'Useful for grilling people,' muttered Old Kent.

Vogler patted Ma Kent on the shoulder and gave her a reassuring smile. He was not a petty man, that's what the smile said – not the sort of oafish bully that would over-react to a blind man's insolence. 'My name is Vogler,' he explained gently. 'Kriminaldirektor Vogler. My job is to investigate subversive activity in these parts. There was trouble here today,' he reminded them softly. 'A terrorist escaped by running across your land. I'm making enquiries about the incident – that's all. It's not that any of you are under suspicion. I will need to make use of this room to interview you all one by one. You have two farm boys?'

'Yes,' agreed Old Kent.

'Where are they?'

'They live in the pillbox,' said Kent. 'There's no room in the house because it was smashed up by— '

'Damaged during the war,' interrupted Ma Kent. It was

not wise to offend the Gestapo.

'Damaged?' growled Old Kent. 'It was shelled from the bloody sea. And where was the Royal Navy? That's what I want to know!'

'It was a big battleship!' squeaked Ma Kent nervously.

'So what?' muttered Old Kent. 'Our navy should have sunk it!'

'I'm sure they tried,' sighed his wife.

'Mrs Kent,' smiled Vogler pleasantly, 'please take one of my men and bring the two boys into the house. Then wait your turn. I will start with your husband.'

'That won't take long,' muttered Old Kent.

'You heard shots?' asked Vogler after Ma Kent had left.

The farmer was uncooperative, but Vogler perfectly understood – having your son killed, your head roasted, your farm ruined, and your country conquered might make a bloke touchy. Kent's papers were in order. He was blind, so he would not have seen anything.

Next he interviewed Ma Kent. She wheezed and coughed and struck Vogler as highly infectious, so the interview was short. The only information he got from her was that her dead son had been called Brian.

The file on Honeysuckle Farm was not very thick. Nothing had happened there since the invasion. Vogler consulted it again; the Kents had two boys working on their farm. One was an evacuee – now fourteen years old – by the name of Alfred Scott. The other looked interesting – a twelve-year-old sent by the Ministry of Agriculture and Fisheries, whose father had been involved in the failed attempt to assassinate Hitler in Trafalgar Square. He'd been executed, of course.

'Your name is Alfred Scott?' he asked the older boy when he'd been ushered into the kitchen.

Alfie followed his own advice and gave a very fine impression of a village idiot several bricks short of a load. A puzzled expression spread across his features. His mouth gaped gormlessly. Slowly he pondered the question before his face lit up with understanding.

'Yes sir,' he replied. 'Alfred,' he said. 'Alfred Scott.' He nodded happily.

'Can you confirm that you were driving the tractor when you heard shots this morning, and that Mr Kent was with you?'

'Yes, sir,' confirmed Alfie after a thoughtful pause. 'We were ploughing Green Meadow, sir.'

'Green Meadow is some distance from the sea?'

'What?'

'The field you were ploughing – it is far away from where your friend Benedict was working?'

'Quite far, sir.'

'But you heard shooting?'

'I think so, sir.'

'And has Benedict talked to you about what happened?'

'He don't talk much, sir. He lives in a world of his own.'

'Very well, Alfred. That will do. Send in the other boy – Benedict Dingle Flint.'

Vogler was sitting by the stove, the Rayburn, which Ma Kent had riddled and raked until it radiated a warm and cheerful glow, rather like Vogler himself. He rose from his chair as soon as Flint crept into the room and greeted the boy with a warm and cheerful smile. *Nothing to worry about,* that's what the smile said.

The Gestapo man had unbuttoned his leather coat and placed his Tyrolean hat on the kitchen table next to the teapot. He shook Flint by the hand.

'So,' he smiled. 'You must be Benedict.'

'Yes,' replied the boy nervously.

'Good,' said Vogler with a merry twinkle. 'Sit yourself down,' he pulled a chair towards the stove, 'and tell me about yourself.'

'I live in the pillbox with Alfie,' explained Flint. 'It's a Type 28.'

'A Type 28?'

'Yes.'

'And your dad? What can you tell me about him?' Vogler had taken out his pipe and was stuffing it with tobacco.

'My dad?'

'Yes.'

'He . . . he's dead.'

'What was he like?'

'He used to read to me.'

'Bedtime stories?'

But Flint could not reply. There *had* been bedtime stories when he'd been little – brilliant bedtimes in his snug bedroom at Hornbeams, Willow Way. Flint remembered his dad standing on one leg, closing one eye and hooting like a loon. *'And hast thou slain the Jabberwock? Come to my arms, my beamish boy!'* Then he'd given his little son a hug – and this had been done very much in the style of a friendly bear hugging his cub.

But Flint's dad had been hunted down and shot.

Then they'd come for his mother.

Vogler waited until the sobbing subsided. 'You were working down by the sea this morning?'

'Yes.'

'What were you doing?'

'Spreading dung.'

'What did you see?'

'I was standing near the cart forking dung. I wasn't facing the sea. I was looking the other way. I heard shots – and I turned round and I saw this lady running down the field with no shoes on. She must have kicked them off – so she could run faster – and there were soldiers chasing after her.'

'Did she see you?'

'She must have done. I was standing by the cart in the middle of the field.'

'The middle of the field?'

'Yes.'

'Did she run towards you?'

'No – she ran past.'

'Did she say anything to you?'

'No.'

'Was she holding anything?'

'I don't think so.'

Vogler's pipe was alight now. He puffed at it like a friendly uncle and gave the boy one of his sympathetic smiles. 'Good,' he murmured. 'Excellent – that puts you in the clear. You may go, Benedict. You may return to your Type 28.' He relaxed, puffing contentedly, and watched as the boy jumped off his chair and darted to the door. 'Just one thing before you go. The soldiers who were giving chase – they reported that when they entered the field the suspect was running in an odd direction.' He paused to let this sink in.

It sank in.

'They say she was running away from your cart – not past it.' He watched the boy with a kindly expression on his warm and cheerful face. 'And one of our patrols reported that there was a fire tonight down on the beach,' he continued gently. 'Did you light that fire?'

'Yes.'

'Why?'

'To keep warm – and to attract fish.'

'Attract fish?'

'Yes.'

Vogler fiddled with his pipe. It was a Sherlock Holmes-style Calabash pipe, so it took a lot of fiddling with. 'OK.' He looked up cheerfully. 'The terrorist was seen running from your cart, and a few hours later you light a fire near to where you met her. A suspicious sort of person might conclude, Benedict, that you were burning something

21

important. Do you know what that means?'

'No.'

'It means trouble!'

Flint felt dizzy. The room seemed to darken. He felt the man's hand on his shoulder, gently pushing – guiding – taking control. All the way out of the house – through the back kitchen where Alfie watched wide-eyed and appalled – all the way to the waiting Mercedes 260 D – Flint was led in a daze. The two soldiers followed them. *Only one of them is armed,* Flint realised. *The other one must be the driver.*

Vogler had his hat on now, the one with the feather, and was still smoking his pipe. He settled himself into the back seat of the Mercedes beside Flint. The soldiers took their places in the front. The car started, the headlights shone, and they were away.

Flint concentrated on unimportant things: the smell of pipe smoke, petrol and leather; the milk churns waiting for the milk lorry; the new moon.

'A wishing moon,' remarked Vogler in his warm and friendly tone. 'Did you make a wish, Benedict?'

Flint could not reply. He knew that they were on their way to the local Gestapo HQ – how many other suspects had been taken there in the same Mercedes 260 D, and had any of them ever come back?

They'll shoot me, like they shot Dad! he thought. *But they'll torture me first! What if I betray Alfie? He helped burn the book!*

Vogler was still talking, his voice a friendly drone, but

Flint could only think about what was going to happen to him. He knew he'd crack under the pain – he'd let everyone down – especially his dad.

He did not hear the bomb. He did not see the road erupt into a cascade of earth and tarmac, or feel the car tumbling through the air.

He saw a blinding light – and that was all.

Vogler survived. He was thrown clear of the spinning car and landed with a sickening smack onto the road, then the Mercedes landed on top of him. The bandits assumed he was dead; they didn't bother to shoot him, but the truth was that the car had bounced before it had rolled.

Vogler was unconscious but alive when the army arrived.

There was no hospital for German officers for thirty miles, so he was rushed to the local cottage hospital, where they patched him up as best they could. He had a private room – which was only right for a Gestapo man of his rank – and that room was under armed guard, as you'd expect.

The guard was Soldat Hans Holzbock from Lower Silesia. Hans was nineteen years old. He'd worked for his father's building firm until he was seventeen, but now he was in the army. That was a shame – he'd rather be back in Silesia drinking beer and taking Beatrix to dances. Hans was worried because he'd had no letter from her for six weeks, and that could only mean one thing: someone else was taking her dancing.

A nurse bustled down the corridor. She was pretty and petite, with bright eyes, and glossy dark hair pinned under her nurse's hat. She gave Hans a mischievous smile. He was on guard but, even so, Hans pretended to snap to attention before giving her a mock salute. The nurse laughed. Hans could see she liked him – and this was very good news, because she was *so* beautiful. He smiled shyly and tried to think of something to say. Hans had an English phrase book so he could ask the way to Buckingham Palace, but he could not chat up girls.

He stood in front of Vogler's door and went quickly through his English vocabulary.

'Me Hans,' he announced. She thought that was really funny.

'You Hans,' she giggled, 'me Jane!'

'You Jane?'

'Me Jane.' She poked him playfully in the ribs and opened the door. 'See you soon.' She winked and disappeared into the private room.

The door closed.

The nurse walked quickly up to Vogler's bed. She pulled back one of his eyelids to check he was still unconscious. Then, carefully and methodically, she set about murdering him.

She held a cloth soaked in diethyl ether over the Gestapo man's mouth and nose. His walrus moustache tickled her hand, but she held the lethal cloth in place for several long minutes. She'd have held it there longer – much longer – if the door had not started to open. She sprang away from the bed, and was busy with a bedpan when a German officer with thick pebble glasses stepped into the room. The nurse gave him a brisk nod and a quick smile as she brushed past him, holding the bedpan in front of her.

The nurse had been highly trained – she was an expert in sabotage and assassination. She'd flirted her way into Vogler's room and bluffed her way out again. Now she was glancing at her watch – time to get moving! What was it the local bandits wanted her to do next – something about a boy?

3

'**W**e gave him a shot of morphine,' said a man's voice in Flint's dream. 'There are morphine kits in the first-aid pack. Only I think they're meant for adults.'

'Of course they're meant for adults!' cried Flint's mum. She was swinging in the swing seat on the terrace at Hornbeams, Willow Way. 'You gave him about twice as much as you should have! But he's not dead. He's still breathing and he's got a pulse.'

'What are you talking about?' asked Flint.

'Nothing – nothing at all. Go back to sleep.'

'But I'm not asleep. I'm playing with my cars.'

The nurse looked anxiously down at the unconscious

form of Benedict Dingle Flint. 'Right,' she said to Aka, 'let's get him to Doc Bolt!'

Flint opened his eyes.

'He's awake!' cried an excited voice. A girl with dark eyes was leaning over him.

'Don't pester him!' called a man's voice.

'I'm not pestering!' replied the girl indignantly. 'I'm not, am I?' she asked Flint.

He closed his eyes again and wondered if he was still dreaming. Eventually he shook his head.

'He says I'm NOT pestering him!' yelled the girl.

Heavy steps ascended wooden stairs and approached Flint's bed. The girl was pushed unceremoniously aside, and a white-haired man with a pale face, a twisted grin and an eagle nose peered down at him.

'How do you feel?' asked the stranger. 'Your leg's broken,' he said without giving Flint time to reply. 'It's been taped to a splint. I had no plaster for a cast. Try not to move it.'

The pale face disappeared, the heavy footsteps receded, and the girl was gazing down at him again. 'I'm Alice,' she told him. 'Would you like a glass of Lucozade? We've got a crate of it.'

Flint remembered Lucozade; his mum had bought it from the Home and Colonial Stores whenever he was ill. He attempted to nod his bruised head, but it was too painful, so he murmured, 'Yes,' and the girl scampered away. He listened as her feet rattled down a flight of wooden stairs.

Where is this place? he asked himself. *And how did I get here?*

A few minutes later Alice returned to his bedside with a glass in her hand. She helped him sit up, propping a pillow behind his throbbing head, and gently raised the glass to his lips. Flint sipped and glanced about. They seemed to be in an attic stuffed to the rafters with weapons.

'They're German,' explained Alice, seeing him look. 'Captured – but you must know all about it.'

'Me?'

'Yes. After all, you're in the Resistance.'

Flint didn't argue. If this young girl with the sweet smile and the dark eyes was under the impression he was a hero of the British Resistance, that was fine by him, even if the sight of all the weapons was disturbing.

'Tumbleweed brought you in,' Alice was telling him. 'She said you'd been arrested by the Gestapo. I suppose you're not allowed to say why.' She gazed at him expectantly.

'No,' replied Flint, wondering who Tumbleweed was, and why – and how, and when – she'd 'brought him in'. 'I don't remember anything about it. One minute I was at Honeysuckle Farm and the next I'm here talking to you.'

'Can't you even tell me about the exploding rats?'

'Exploding rats?'

'The Resistance is famous for them,' claimed Alice. 'Grandpa's in the patrol, but he never talks to me about

28

them.' She settled herself down on the end of Flint's bed. It was a folding camp bed, so it took a lot of shifting about until she was comfortable. 'He never talks to me about any of that stuff, and nor do any of the others.'

Flint closed his eyes. He wanted to sleep, but did not want to miss anything the girl might say. 'Grandpa used my hockey stick for your splint,' she was telling him. 'Are you really called Flint?'

'Yes – Benedict Flint.'

'Benedict – that's nice. You look as if you're called Benedict – apart from the bruise. It's funny to think you're a terrorist. Did you know Enid Blyton escaped to New York?'

He shook his head.

'All her books are set in America now. Tumbleweed's just given me *Five Go West* – I got as far as page 19 while I was waiting for you to come round. Tumbleweed's very mysterious,' she continued, 'as well as very pretty. I expect she goes to America all the time. I expect that's where she gets her stockings and her lipsticks. Would you like a chicken sandwich? Or would you prefer a boiled egg?'

'Where am I?'

'In the attic.'

'What attic?'

'The Bolt Hole attic!' She waved a hand in the general direction of the rafters. 'This is my grandpa's house – it's where the patrol store stuff.'

'Stuff?'

'Explosives and stuff – it's a safe house. The Gestapo won't find you here.'

Gestapo, thought Flint, remembering the scent of pipe tobacco. He closed his eyes again and attempted to work out just how a house stuffed with explosives could be described as safe.

'Grandpa's the quartermaster for Dart Patrol,' the girl was telling him eagerly.

Patrol? thought Flint before drifting off to sleep. *What's she talking about?*

Two days went by – two days in which Alice watched him carefully with her huge, dark eyes – two days during which he'd drift in and out of sleep. Unconnected snatches of the girl's conversation would greet him whenever he woke. He'd hear her say things like, 'Grandpa's nicked some honey – would you like some?' Then a heavier tread on the wooden stairs would wake him, and it would be Doc Bolt wanting to examine his leg. The old fellow had received his medical training on a Wednesday afternoon in 1916, and Flint had the distinct impression that he found his broken leg disappointing. 'Nothing for me to do,' he'd sigh. 'No putrefaction; no rotting flesh. I took the trouble to breed a bucketful of maggots especially for you.'

'Maggots?'

'Maggots are partial to pus. They eat it like you'd eat ice cream. By sprinkling maggots on to a septic wound you make them happy. They feast on necrotic flesh. They chomp away, those hungry little fellows, until only healthy tissue is left.'

'Grandpa's more used to bullets,' Alice had added. 'He pulls them out with his special tweezers.'

The Resistance hero had sipped his way through a bottle of Lucozade and two bottles of Robinsons Barley Water before he could be tempted to try a sandwich. This was three days after he'd been brought in. Alice scampered down the stairs and returned with two slices of generously buttered white bread, holding thick slices of cold chicken and pheasant with a dash of cranberry sauce. Food like this was a luxury in 1942, but Doc Bolt's strange house seemed full of luxuries. Flint bit into the sandwich and chewed gratefully.

'It's not just chicken,' explained the girl. 'It's pheasant too. Grandpa's good at poaching pheasants. He has the knack.'

'Knack?'

'He has the knack for all sorts of things,' she told him earnestly, 'especially looting.'

For his first two weeks at the Bolt Hole Flint was confined to the attic, but the day came when Doc Bolt ripped off the gaffer tape, returned the hockey-stick splint to its rightful owner, and informed Flint that he could limp downstairs. Alice guided him gently to what she called the parlour and sat him down on the settee so that his legs were stretched out in front of him. He looked around the snug and comfy room. This was better than the pillbox or the back kitchen at Honeysuckle Farm: a glowing log fire, huge leather chairs, the vast settee, pictures of galloping horses and ships in full sail. A dog the size of a small pony lay asleep on the hearthrug.

'That's Ironside,' Alice told him. 'He's very old. He's an elkhound. For hunting elk,' she added in case Flint wasn't quite bright enough to work that out for himself. 'That's an elk,' she said, pointing at the chimney breast, where the head of a stuffed moose gazed calmly down at them through a pair of dusty glass eyes. Flint nodded politely, happily aware that Alice was watching him with round-eyed wonder. *It makes a nice change,* he told himself, *to be treated like a hero instead of a startled canary.* That reminded him of Alfie. *I hope he's OK,* he thought anxiously. *I hope they've not roped him into the Resistance, and he's still alive and safe and living in the pillbox.*

Ironside the elkhound thumped his tail. His ears quivered. His nose twitched. He recognised Alice's special Alice scent – a delicate blend of Sunlight soap and the perfume spray that Tumbleweed had given her – but there was nothing in the least delicate about Flint's smell. The huge hound snuffed the air with sleepy interest. *A human boy,* he worked out without looking, *smelling strongly of dung.*

'Would you like a bath?' asked Alice hopefully.

'Yes,' replied Flint. 'I haven't had a bath for years!'

'Really?' the girl replied sweetly. 'I'd never have guessed!'

When Flint eventually returned to his place on the settee Ironside checked him out again. The young visitor still smelt strongly of human boy, but now there were strong traces of soap, toothpaste and mint humbugs too. Flint in turn could detect the aged hound's distinctive old-dog smell as it mingled pleasantly with the subtle scents of the Bolt Hole – wood smoke and candle wax, oil lamps and casseroles.

'You say I was arrested?' said Flint.

'That's what Tumbleweed said. She said you were in the Gestapo car that Aka and the others blew up – they didn't know you were in it.'

'But why was I in the car?'

'Because you're in the Resistance. That's what the Gestapo does – arrest bandits. But don't worry, they're not going to find you out here. The thing about the Bolt Hole,' Alice explained, 'is that it's in bandit country – the Germans hardly ever patrol round here. They stick to the main roads and they guard the railway lines, but they keep clear of the woods and the fields, and if they're crazy enough to venture down one of our lanes they get ambushed. That's why the Resistance stores stuff here. Grandpa looks after it for them.' She nodded. 'And I look after Grandpa.'

'Have you got a mum and dad?' asked Flint. As soon as he'd blurted out this blunt question he realised he'd been just a little insensitive. He watched guiltily as Alice's dark eyes filled with tears. But she didn't want to talk about it.

'My dad was executed,' he told her, anxious to change the subject. 'Then they arrested my mum.'

Alice's wet eyes opened wider. She stretched out a hand and squeezed one of his. 'So,' she said, 'you don't know where she is?'

He shook his head.

'Or if she's alive or dead?'

'No.'

'That's better,' Alice assured him. 'That's better than knowing she's dead.' It was as if she spoke from experience.

'Yes,' agreed Flint. 'I suppose it is.'

'Oh, it is,' she told him firmly. 'Because it gives you hope!'

She gave his hand another squeeze.

4

Queen Elizabeth had been a fourteen-year-old princess when she'd arrived in Newfoundland just a week after the fall of London. Now that her father had been executed, she was queen.

'Pretender?' she asked in her posh, royal voice. 'What's that?'

'It's what the Germans are calling you, ma'am.'

'You mean they're saying I'm pretending to be queen?'

'Yes, ma'am, I fear so.'

Lord Max Blade was the head of the British government in exile – and the only one of Winston Churchill's war cabinet still alive. He was a Canadian, which was why Churchill had chosen him to take the precious princess to Newfoundland shortly before the Battle of London. Now he was in the royal Nissen hut at St John's, smiling warily at the new queen's three huge Newfoundland dogs. They were young too – no more than overgrown puppies. They raced around the orphan queen's feet, wagging their tails.

Max Blade spoke to Elizabeth in the special kind-but-firm coaxing voice he always used with her. It was important that she did exactly as she was told, but he couldn't actually order her about. 'It is because the Germans are saying you're not the real queen that we must have your coronation as soon as possible,' he advised the girl firmly.

'But I'm in mourning!' the child almost wept. This was true: both her parents had been shot.

'That won't stop your uncle getting crowned next month.' Lord Blade fixed the girl with his sharp eyes. She had to be brave; she had to measure up. 'And *his* coronation will be in Westminster Abbey with all the right regalia. We must beat him to it, ma'am. We need news-reels of our brave young queen being crowned in a no-fuss ceremony. We must show her looking sad but noble as she's driven off in an open carriage escorted by the Royal Canadian Dragoons. Then, marching behind, we'll have detachments from the Eighth Army, still in their desert uniforms, looking determined and tough.'

He rocked on his heels, looking determined and tough himself. It was impossible to disagree with Lord Blade –

his sharp tongue could cut you to shreds, which was why they called him The Razor.

'Oh,' she gasped. 'I suppose that's right.'

'It is, ma'am. We need to establish you in the eyes of the world as the *real* monarch. And then we need to eliminate the opposition.' Lord Blade smiled a smile so wide it seemed to meet itself at the back of his head.

'Eliminate?' The girl's eyes widened. 'You mean you're going to assassinate my uncle?'

'He's a traitor – him and his fascist queen.' Lord Blade hissed out the words. 'And the Germans are using the pair of them to legitimise their puppet government. This is why they must both be taken out of the game.'

The girl's lip trembled as she watched Lord Blade give a curt bow and make for the door. She had been in St John's for two years now. They'd sent her little sister somewhere else. Sometimes she received letters from her, letters with pictures of kittens, but without an address.

Her Britannic Majesty Queen Elizabeth the Second knew that Newfoundland was the right place for her to be, and she could understand that it made perfect sense for Princess Margaret to be hidden away somewhere else – even if it made her cry every night.

St John's was where what was left of the British Army was based – along with several other armies from Canada, Australia, New Zealand, India, and Newfoundland itself. It was where the British North Atlantic fleet had its continental base. That's why she had to be there.

That's why she had to be brave, and do her duty, and wave and smile, and never once show she was scared. She was the queen, and if the enemy succeeded in assassinating her – why, then, her little sister would be taken out from wherever she was hiding, and she'd be queen instead.

The three dogs looked up at her. 'What do you lot want?' she asked. 'Would it be a WALK, by any chance?'

The dogs wagged and scampered. They shot out of the door as soon it was opened for them, and the teen-queen darted after them. She was alone apart from the three excited dogs as she had the royal Nissen hut all to herself. She could have lived in Government House, but Lord Blade had advised against it. 'You must not look as if you're living in luxury,' he'd advised. 'Leave that to your aunt.' The traitor queen was famous for her extravagance.

Elizabeth had just turned sharply down the concrete path that led away from her 'tin palace' when she saw that her three dogs were prancing round a pretty young woman with bright, sparkling eyes and dark hair pinned under her hat – her *captain's* hat.

'Sorry!' squeaked the queen. She was very polite; she'd been very carefully brought up.

The pretty young woman in the uniform practically jumped out of her socks – not that she was wearing socks. This was always happening to Elizabeth; when your head's on the stamps and your picture is always in the papers, people tend to jump out of their socks when they run into you. The young woman looked so flustered, as if she was wondering whether to curtsey or salute. The teen-queen watched in polite silence as the young woman bobbed a quick curtsey and made a swift salute before scuttling down the path to Hut 573.

Golly – Hut 573, the queen noted with awe. *She must be in the SOE!*

Lord Blade had told her that the Special Operations Executive made MI6 look like a bunch of milksops. Apparently it was SOE that had assassinated the Vice-President of Vichy France, and the Nazi governor of Poland. It was SOE that had blown up the German nuclear research plant and thrown the German ambassador to the United States of America off Brooklyn Bridge.

Above all, it was SOE that ran the Resistance.

'She must be a secret agent,' she said to her dogs. 'The lucky thing!'

Hut 573 was warm and bright. May sunshine shone through the windows. Important chaps with be-ribboned chests glanced up as Tumbleweed slipped into the room. A general looked at his watch. A colonel glared. But mostly they ignored her, and concentrated on the cuttings and photographs of Queen Wallis that had been pinned to the corkboard.

Tumbleweed saw her boss, a dapper, debonair man with mischievous eyes. He looked stylish and suave and terribly amusing. He beckoned her towards him with an easy smile and nodded at the bigwigs clustered round the corkboard.

'They want it to look like an accident,' he said.

'Of course,' she replied, looking crisp and efficient. 'Of course they do!'

5

'The High-Ups are all in Newfoundland,' explained Doc. 'They're the ones that give the orders. Their agents come and go, like the lovely Tumbleweed – they bring in new codes and stuff – make sure we're not slacking.' He cupped his hands to light a German cigarette and puffed contentedly. 'Fell off a train,' he chuckled.

It was just after breakfast on a bright new day, and Flint was happy being useful; he was lending Doc a hand. The two of them were out in the yard behind the Bolt Hole, checking stores. There were old stables and a big double garage back there, and they were stuffed with stuff – tins of dried egg, sacks of rice and flour, instant mashed potato – that sort of stuff.

Stuff you could eat!

'Yes,' continued Doc, blowing a smoke ring. 'The Resistance is made up of patrols, and SOE gives them their orders. There are patrols all over the country from Land's End to John O'Groats – they call themselves bandits.'

'So where exactly *is* bandit country?' asked Flint. 'Alice said we were in bandit country, but it doesn't look any different from anywhere else – fields and woods and countryside.'

'Bandit country is anywhere the Huns are scarce,' explained Doc, 'and the Resistance can more or less do as they please. The Germans don't have enough soldiers to keep the whole country under their thumbs now they've invaded Russia, so they concentrate on the towns and cities. Alice was right – they hardly ever bother us round here so *this* is bandit country. I'm quartermaster to a patrol of bandits; I store munitions for them and I forage for food. They creep about at night doing heroic bandit stuff, but I'm too old for that, so that's why I'm their quartermaster – and you are now a quartermaster's apprentice. Tonight's the night, Benedict – the night you engage.'

'Engage?' gasped Flint. 'Engage with what?'

'The enemy!'

Hans glared despondently into the dark and wondered uneasily if he was being watched. Most nights of the year he would be guarding something boring – last week the Gestapo officer at the hospital and tonight railway sidings. There were always goods wagons standing in the sidings, and looters were strangely drawn to them.

He was on guard duty with Wolfgang who was practically a midget. (With his helmet on he looked like a tortoise on stilts.) They were standing on a bridge, which was so caked in soot it was called Black Bridge, looking down on to the railway.

'He's mad!' Wolfgang muttered.

'What?' asked Hans, who had been thinking about the pretty nurse and wondering if he'd ever see her again. It had stopped raining, but it was still cold and dark – too dark to see Wolfgang's face. 'Who's mad?'

'Who do you think?' growled Wolfgang. 'Adolf Hitler – that's who! They're getting stronger every day.' Wolfgang enjoyed moaning about the war. In his opinion, defeat was inevitable and death certain. It was only a matter of avoiding it for as long as possible.

'Who's getting stronger?'

'The Resistance!' sighed Wolfgang. 'And they've still got their navy, and it's still ten times bigger than ours – and they've still got an army!'

'What army?'

'They had armies all over the planet at the start of the war. And where are they now?' Wolfgang waited for an answer, but Hans did not reply. 'Thousands of them are over here!' Wolfgang hissed. 'Out there!' He pointed into the dark towards bandit country. 'And the rest of them are in Canada sharpening their bayonets! I'll tell you this for nothing – your chances of ever getting back to Silesia are ten thousand to one!'

But Hans was not listening. He was staring into the darkness. 'Look!' he whispered.

Wolfgang glanced down the railway track. '*Mein Gott!*' he whistled. 'What's that?'

It was just the sort of stunt Flint pulled off in his daydreams, but he wasn't dreaming. He could feel the rail track cold, wet and hard under his thigh. He could smell the tar and creosote from the sleepers. He knew that there were two guards on the bridge, and that they'd see him as soon as he lit the match.

Quickly he pulled the rags out of his pocket, unscrewed the bottle and soaked them in petrol. It spilt over his hand, cold and toxic, but he was on his feet now, prepared for flight. He fumbled for a match and struck it, but the matchstick broke. Flint froze: if the guards had seen the spark, their guns would be pointing in his direction, waiting for him to strike again.

In one of his daydreams young Firebrand Flint would have been cool and nonchalant, but in his dreams the enemy always missed. He waited. *Maybe if I change my position,* he calculated desperately. *Move further away.* He picked up the petrol-soaked rags and tiptoed down the line away from the bridge for another 50 yards. *I'll turn my back on them,* he thought, *so they won't see anything until the rags are alight.*

He struck the match and the rags billowed into flame. There were shouts from the bridge. A shot rang out. Flint bolted.

Hans and Wolfgang ran towards the dancing flames under cover of a row of goods wagons. Where the wagons stopped, Wolfgang stopped too. He caught hold of Hans's arm.

'There's no point being a dead hero,' he advised his companion. That was Wolfgang's motto: *Stay alive for as long as you can! They'll get you in the end, but don't let them get you tonight.*

They crouched behind the end wagon and stared down the line towards the flames.

'That's not sabotage,' whispered Hans. 'The fire's not big enough to do any damage.'

They knew what that meant. It meant the fire had been lit to lure them to it.

'They'll be out there, looking down their sights,' muttered Wolfgang, 'waiting for us to step into the fire-light.' He had no intention of walking into a trap. 'We'll stay here,' he hissed, 'under this wagon – out of sight – and we'll be quiet as mice!'

Flint scrambled up the embankment, squeezed through a break in the railings, and made it into Station Road, where he scuttled nervously towards the dark outline of a truck.

Doc Bolt handed Flint a bucket with a length of rope

attached to its handle. 'OK,' he instructed. 'Down you go!'

The railways ran on coal. So did the gas works. So did every house in England, Scotland and Wales. And people could get it absolutely free of charge from railway sidings, so long as they were reckless enough to risk getting shot. The lumps might be on an industrial scale, but that actually made it easier to nick. All it took was a young volunteer to clamber down into the siding, perch himself on top of the heap, load lumps into a bucket, and tug at the rope. Then you'd simply haul up the load, drop the huge lumps into the back of the truck, and chuck the bucket back for more.

Of course, it helped if the apprehensive young volunteer had taken the trouble to light a diversionary fire on the other side of the bridge.

Flint heaved a huge hunk of coal into the bucket. His hands were trembling, his throat was dry, and a swarm of butterflies was looping the loop in his tummy. He tugged at the rope and watched the bucket disappear. There was a grunt, a thump, then the empty bucket came tumbling back.

This was scary. In his dreams he had nerves of steel, and whenever Alice was watching him with her wide, bright eyes he was filled with reckless daring. But Alice was not watching; she was back in the Bolt Hole parlour sipping drinking chocolate and reading *Five Go West* for the second time. He tried not to think of the armed guards and where they might be.

'That's enough!' Doc called eventually. Flint – very much in need of another bath – scrambled back to the truck and clambered into the passenger seat. Doc Bolt crept furtively down the road, looked, listened, and disappeared into the railway siding himself. Flint waited. A sudden clank from below made him jump. If he'd heard that clank, then the guards would have heard it too.

Heavy footsteps approached. Flint felt faint. He had no papers, he was breaking the curfew and he was sitting in a stolen truck piled high with looted coal. Disrupting energy supply was a capital offence. Maybe they'd shoot him there and then.

The sinister footsteps stopped. Something heavy clattered into the truck behind him. The door opened and Doc Bolt swung himself behind the wheel. 'Two crates,' he grinned.

'Two crates of what?'

'God knows. We'll find out when we break them open. Sometimes it's dried egg. Sometimes it's semolina. Once it was *Schinkenwurst*.'

'*Schinkenwurst*?'

'German spam,' explained Doc, releasing the hand-brake and letting the Trojan roll downhill. As soon as they were far enough from the bridge he started the engine, slammed his foot onto the accelerator, and roared out of town heading for bandit country.

Flint sat in the lurching Trojan's cabin and peered anxiously ahead. When Doc struck his lighter he caught sight of his reflection in the windscreen and jumped – he looked like a sketch done in charcoal. His hands were filthy, and since he'd used them to scratch his ears, wipe his nose and push back his hair, he looked like a human badger.

The Bolt Hole had once been a hunting lodge. This was why it was so remote and so far from any road. You could only get to it down green lanes, which was why Doc drove a Trojan Long Bonnet. 'It runs on Tractor Vaporising Oil,' he explained to his apprentice, 'readily available from all local farms, with or without the farmer's consent.'

Doc had not survived with a full belly through the Great War without perfecting his poaching, scrounging and looting skills, and he was happy to pass on his knowledge. He stopped on the way back to give Flint a training session. He drove into a field, fished a sub-machine gun from under a rug, and lamped six rabbits and a lamb.

'All you need,' the expert explained to his apprentice, 'are headlights and a Thompson submachine gun.'

Flint arched his eyebrows in the dark and replied, 'Headlights, a submachine gun and some mint sauce!'

'Mint sauce! Very good!' laughed Doc. He turned the headlights off – it didn't do to draw attention to yourself for too long in bandit country – and cautiously steered the vintage Trojan out of the field with its sidelights dimly illuminating the track. Flint jumped out to close the gate behind them and climbed back into the passenger seat.

'Right,' said Doc, 'we're giving most of what we got

tonight to the patrol.'

'The local bandits?'

'They're busy boys,' explained Doc Bolt. 'And they're usually hungry.'

Flint remembered the young man at the beach. He'd obviously been hungry. 'Where will we find them?' he asked.

'We won't find them. They'll find us.'

This proved to be the case. After a mile of rattling and lurching down the dimly lit lane, Flint was amazed to see glowing pinpoints of red. Doc brought the Trojan to a standstill. One of the tiny red eyes approached, and a familiar face looked into the cabin.

'Evening, Doc – how's tricks?'

It was the bandit from the beach.

'How's the leg?' he asked Flint.

'It was broken,' he replied shyly. 'Doc put it in a splint. It's better now.'

'He doesn't remember anything about what happened,' explained Doc. 'Is that not so, Flinty?' Before Flint could reply, another bandit appeared, leading a carthorse by its bridle.

'Round the back!' called Doc. 'Help yourselves! Pack horse,' he explained to Flint. 'They can get hold of trucks and vans when they want them, but their OB is a long way off-road – so they need horses.'

Flint nodded wisely. He had no idea what an OB was.

'Operational Base,' explained Doc. 'The Nazis send scout planes,' he went on, 'spotter aircraft over bandit country, looking for smoke – but they're too smart for the bastards.'

Flint nodded again. The bandits were breaking open the mysterious crates Doc had looted from the railway siding, and loading the horse's saddle packs with tins. 'Baked beans,' Doc informed him as he squinted into the gloom. 'They'll like that. And dried milk.'

The rabbits were slung across the horse's neck, but the bandits were not interested in the slaughtered lamb.

'We won't be able to eat it all ourselves,' whispered Flint.

'We won't have to. I'll butcher it tomorrow and sell it round the pubs. I've got a cleaver and a special saw. It's the one I use for amputations.'

Doc started the engine, and the Trojan rattled down the lane. Flint yawned and settled his head into the upholstery. He closed his eyes and drifted into sleep.

He was ten years old and climbing the apple tree – the friendly apple tree in the long back garden of Hornbeams, Willow Way, in the county of Surrey.

What I need is a dog, *he was thinking as he swayed in the bare branches.* It would be good to have a dog that could walk on its hind legs – jump through hoops – do special tricks!

There was a noise from the house – half scream, half gasp.

'Benedict!' His mother came rushing out onto the terrace. 'They've shot your dad!' she cried. 'He's dead!'

That had been the last of Flint's happy days. Before that, everything had been snug, secure and certain. After it, nothing was secure, and only death was certain.

There was a sharp knock at the front door. Mrs Flint grabbed her frightened son and tugged him through the French windows. But they were waiting in the back garden. She pulled the boy back into the house, but they'd kicked in the front door. They'd smashed the stained glass. The hall was full of boots and guns.

'Remember me!' she screamed as they bundled her out of the house.

'REMEMBER ME!'

'Mum!' he cried out in his sleep as the Trojan lurched into a pothole and out again, rattling and swaying.

He woke with the dream vivid in his memory.

Where had they taken her?

6

Alice was the first to hear the news. She scampered to the old stables, where Doc Bolt and Flint were busy unloading crates of kippers, tins of jam and canisters of dried egg. It was 10.45 a.m.

'The queen's dead!' she cried excitedly.

'Which one?' Doc looked worried. 'Not the little one?'

'No! Not her! Not the *real* one! The other one!'

'The traitor queen?'

'Yes! I was listening to *Music While You Work*,' explained Alice breathlessly, 'and suddenly there was a news announcement. Queen Wallis was killed in a car crash this morning. It must have happened near here, because she died in the military hospital in Exeter.'

'So,' growled Doc. 'She's met with an accident!' He made a throat-cutting gesture.

Alice's eyes widened. 'They said there were no suspicious circumstances.'

'No suspicious circumstances?' snorted Doc. 'A fascist queen meets with a fatal accident on the edge of bandit country – and "no suspicious circumstances"? Pull the other one!'

'You mean she was murdered?' asked Flint. 'By *our* people?'

Doc tapped the side of his nose with an index finger. 'Don't ask,' he grinned.

The body lay on a slab, its eyes wide open as if in surprise. Someone had identified the corpse by tying a luggage label round one of the big toes: *HRH Queen Wallis*, it said in red ink.

Dr Franz Alfred Six, Gestapo Chief for Occupied English Territory, examined the body. He was a doctor of political science, not a medical doctor, so the examination was brief. 'Cause of death?' he asked.

'Broken neck,' said one of the real doctors. 'It would have been instantaneous.'

Dr Six nodded. 'Right,' he said. 'Now show me the driver.'

'Her driver?'

'No, the one that caused the accident – the idiot in the armoured car.'

Imagine a pair of cartoon ears, blood-red with the sun behind them as he stood in front of a hospital window. Imagine them jutting out from either side of a hairless head. Imagine a rat-like face with fiercely staring eyes, a livid scar zipping down the right cheek. Picture those crazed eyes magnified with frightening intensity by a pair of thick pebble glasses, and you'll have a vague impression of Dr Franz Alfred Six.

They led him to the cubicle where the dead German soldier lay – the driver of the armoured car who'd caused the accident. Dr Six looked at the body critically. 'So what was he playing at?' he asked. 'What was he doing racing out of a side road onto the A30 without stopping?'

The question had been rhetorical; he had not expected an answer, but a young *Kriminalsekretär* in a leather coat spoke up bravely. 'It's easily done,' he replied. 'They drive on the left and we drive on the right.'

Dr Six frowned. The huge eyes behind the pebble glasses glared at the young *Kriminalsekretär*. The armoured car had not been driving on the wrong side of the road; it had shot into the main road without warning and smacked into the royal Rolls-Royce. He turned scornfully from the *Kriminalsekretär* and consulted the note he'd received in his London office. *Queen Wallis*, it had informed him bleakly, *was involved in a fatal crash on the A30 at 9.36 GMT between Chard and Honiton. She was on her way to open a new wing at the Royal Devon and Exeter Hospital for soldiers suffering from burns, when her vehicle was struck head on by a Leichter Panzerspähwagen emerging from a side road.*

Dr Six peered at the driver's bruised and battered head, then examined the dilated pupils of the dead, staring eyes. 'Conduct a full post-mortem,' he instructed the doctors. 'You'll find he was drugged.' But he was sniffing now – what was that elusive scent? Perfume – subtle, expensive perfume – not cheap scent.

The Gestapo chief leaned closer. What was that on the dead man's collar?

Lipstick!

A woman was involved in this case – a cultivated woman with expensive perfume. Dr Six examined the driver's pockmarked face. It was ugly, the eyes slightly crossed, the teeth a faded shade of yellow. Why would a woman with good taste have anything to do with such a dismal specimen?

He made no comment. He had his suspicions as to how the driver had ended up drugged and smacking into the A30 at exactly the right time to kill the queen, but he kept them to himself. The last thing he wanted Hitler to know was that security in Occupied English Territory was so lax that SOE had been able to assassinate the puppet queen.

That was a little secret he'd keep to himself.

Alice rushed into the yard the morning after the death of Queen Wallis. 'You mustn't go into the kitchen,' she told Flint, 'because Tumbleweed's having a bath. She arrived late last night, and she's brought me *Five Go to Yellowstone Park*.'

'Who?'

'Tumbleweed – the lady who brought you here. She wants to see you as soon as she's dressed and put on her make-up and dabbed her pulse points with Taboo. Tumbleweed's really funny and really pretty. You'll like her!'

Flint sniffed as he made his way to the parlour to wait. Mixed with the familiar Bolt Hole scents of old dog and candle wax was a whiff of something romantic and mysterious. Something that reminded him of home – of Hornbeams, Willow Way. He sniffed some more. The scent reminded him of his mother – she'd smelt like that the night Dad had taken her to the tennis club ball.

A handbag was sitting on a low table in the hall, and a fur coat had been tossed carelessly over the back of a chair. Ironside thumped his tail on the hearthrug as Flint sank into one of the leather chairs and waited.

'She's down in the cellar checking explosives,' announced Alice half an hour later. 'I think she has a job for you. It's bound to be terribly dangerous!' Her bright eyes gleamed.

Flint jumped off the rocking chair, tripped over Ironside, and pranced anxiously out of the Bolt Hole parlour under the impassive gaze of the stuffed elk. He'd never been into the cellar; he had no idea how to find it. All he knew about Tumbleweed was that she'd '*brought him in*'. Since he had no memory of the roadside bomb, this information made her seem totally mysterious.

'Benedict!' called a welcoming voice as he cautiously descended into the lamp-lit gloom of the cellar. 'You're looking *so* much better!'

The mysterious, bright-eyed Tumbleweed gave him a merry smile, and then – because he stood transfixed in shy silence – a friendly hug. He swayed, stunned by the scent of Taboo and the feel of her soft wool-and-angora dress, until she laughed and kissed him lightly on the top of his head.

Flint felt very much as he might have felt if he'd been hugged and kissed by a film star. Maybe Tumbleweed *was* a film star! She certainly looked like one. He could not take his eyes off her, and he had the strange impression that he'd seen her somewhere before.

Actually, he *had* seen her before. On 3 January 1940 – six months before the invasion – the Flints of Hornbeams, Willow Way, had climbed into their Morris Oxford and driven into Guildford to see *Aladdin*. That was where Flint had seen Tumbleweed – not that he recognised her – she'd been Aladdin's girlfriend, the lovely Princess Lotus Blossom. She'd been the one who had sung 'When You Wish upon a Star' and 'Over the Rainbow'.

'Now,' she giggled. 'We're going to have some fun with the Hun. How good are you at climbing trees?'

Flint remembered the apple tree in the long back garden of Hornbeams, Willow Way. 'Not bad,' he managed to reply. 'Not bad at all!'

*

And so it was that, after a light lunch of scrambled eggs, fried tomatoes and spam, Flint shot up the tall oak that Tumbleweed had selected for him.

'Most impressive!' she called. 'Benedict Dingle Flint,' she cried, 'part boy, part gibbon! Now let down the rope and pull up the equipment!' She lashed the end of Flint's rope round the handle of a large basket and watched thoughtfully as the boy pulled it up into the branches. 'Tie it up!' she instructed. 'We don't want you dropping it – that's expensive kit you've got up there!'

Flint followed her instructions, and soon he was peering through the tender green leaves at the winding country road below him. They were about three miles west of the Bolt Hole, surrounded by fields he was unfamiliar with. He directed his attention to the radio and spoke anxiously into the microphone. The Gestapo monitored the airways and could locate where clandestine radio messages were coming from, and this knowledge made Flint just a tiny bit concerned.

The lady I saw running through Three Corner Field must have been located by one of their locator vans, he thought anxiously. *The Gestapo must have tracked down her radio signals and discovered her secret radio out-station.*

Tumbleweed had told him that the young woman who'd told him to burn her code book had been a 'Secret Sweetie' – that was what the bandits called the hush-hush young women who were flown in from Newfoundland to run secret radio stations for the Resistance. The Gestapo particularly enjoyed hunting down, torturing and executing the Secret Sweeties, which was why they were issued with suicide capsules.

Flint's stomach was churning now, and his hair was wet with sweat. He had *not* been issued with a suicide capsule. If things did not go to plan when the Gestapo tracked his signal down, there would be what Doc described as *unpleasantness.* Flint could just about face being executed – OK, he'd probably wet himself and snivel a bit – but the idea of torture terrified him. He thought about the Gestapo listening stations with their towering radio masts, the high-tech tracker vans designed to home in on signals and surprise the secret operators.

His mouth was dry; his voice croaked as he read out the words: 'CROCODILE, CROOK, CRUNCH.' He paused, swallowed, licked his lips, turned a page and read: 'DENSE, DENTAL, FROST, FROWN.'

Tumbleweed had selected the oak tree in which Flint was perched because it was in an 'exposed and vulnerable position', which meant that it was on top of a hill and could be seen for miles. What made things worse was that the oak was not yet in full leaf. It was true that she'd camouflaged him by painting his face a light shade of apple green and plonking the Bolt Hole tea cosy over his fair hair, but he was still somewhat conspicuous.

Flint checked his list of words and croaked into the mike: 'GHASTLY, GESTAPO, GOON.'

The nearest Gestapo listening station was attached to Camp Vigilant, about ten miles away. It bristled with barbed wire and radio masts, and it boasted bombproof bunkers and a jumble of reinforced concrete buildings. There was an airstrip just long enough for spotter planes to land and take off, and at the heart of Camp Vigilant stood Castle Bullstock, where they'd once held summer fetes and served cream teas.

'It's a new code,' muttered a signals corporal as he listened to an enemy radio message. They were in the castle hall with the heraldic chimney piece – this was where the listeners listened.

Dr Six leaned forward alertly – his bat ears gave him acute hearing. He held up one of his pale, limp hands and stuck a finger into the air. 'That's not a woman's voice,' he hissed. 'That's a child!'

'A boy,' agreed the corporal.

Dr Six nodded. 'Bring the little fellow in!' he murmured. 'I'd like a word with him!' He laid one limp hand upon another as if in prayer and shifted his feet until he stood in front of the window. He liked to have the light behind him. He was like Napoleon in that respect.

Flint was reading, 'INVENT, INWARD, IOTA,' when he heard the approaching Gestapo tracking vehicle followed by a truck of soldiers – a unit of the Waffen-SS. What had Tumbleweed told him? *Keep going,* she'd said. *Keep reading. Don't run! We'll keep you safe! Everything will be tickety-boo!*

He was certainly not going to desert his post – not with Tumbleweed watching from the ditch below. He thumbed desperately through the book. She'd marked all the pages she wanted him to read from. He'd asked her who'd be listening apart from the Gestapo, but she'd just murmured, 'Don't ask!' Alice had told him that it was one of Tumbleweed's favourite phrases.

Don't ask!

At least I'm camouflaged, thought Flint, adjusting the tea cosy. Now he could see the tracker van speeding down the road towards him; behind it roared the truck full of Nazi soldiers. *I bet they're the ones who chased that lady through Three Corner,* thought Flint. *That's what this is all about. Tumbleweed wants revenge. She's set a trap, and I'm the bait!*

He kept reading until an explosion sent the tracker van vaulting into the sky. Up it shot – down it tumbled – to land smack in the bomb crater for the truck to crash into. Flint saw all this happening – saw the van rise and crash – long before he heard the echoing bang. It was the same with the shooting – before the shocked soldiers could get out from the wreckage, bandits opened fire on them at close range from behind the hedge. Flint saw the bodies twist and drop before he even heard the shots.

Shooting from behind thick, solid English hedges, the local bandits massacred the shell-shocked soldiers with impunity. A whole platoon of German infantry was gunned down, with no British casualties.

Apart from Alfie.

He'd been hit in the hand – his right hand. Flint hadn't seen it happen, and Alfie himself was confused. One minute he'd been firing on the enemy, the next his sub-machine gun had spun out of his grasp and there'd been blood running down his arm – lots of it.

Flint watched, appalled, as they laid him on the grass and Tumbleweed applied a tourniquet. He scrambled down from the tree and raced towards his wounded friend. The mysterious young man with the keen eyes, who'd helped himself to their fish at Flat Rock, pushed him back.

Alfie held up the blood-soaked bandage. *I'm a real bandit,* the gesture seemed to say, *not a mere decoy.*

'I've been recruited!' he informed Flint proudly. 'I've taken the oath!'

'Shut up!' growled the keen-eyed young man – he was called Aka, Flint remembered.

'I like the tea cosy!' Alfie was trying to be brave – and succeeding. A smile lit up his pale face as they bunged him into the back of a van. Tumbleweed scrambled in beside him and slammed the doors. Then they drove him to the Bolt Hole.

It was a case for the tweezers – and the maggots.

Maybe the saw.

Flint watched the van speed away until a familiar voice told him to look sharp. Aka was the only one left on the scene – all the others had melted away – and he was look-ing at Flint with a sharp, calculating air.

'You did well,' he said. 'And Doc says you've been a great help to him.'

Flint got the impression that Aka never said much, but

when he did it was worth listening to. He felt flattered. Tumbleweed had told him that Aka had been a bandit since the invasion. Before that, he'd been a bandit in waiting – specially selected, specially trained, specially equipped to fight a secret war of terror.

Flint glanced at the bandit leader anxiously. He was not in uniform, although some of the others had been in faded, tattered battledress. Some of them had even been wearing standard British helmets festooned with foliage, but Aka seemed to prefer a brown woollen forage hat. His face had been smeared with mud, although he could have saved himself the trouble, since he looked as if he hadn't shaved for a month.

'The Huns will be here in force soon,' he warned Flint. 'Let's go!' He led the boy south. 'I'm sending you back to Honeysuckle Farm.'

'But I'm Doc's apprentice!' cried Flint. He thought wistfully of the Bolt Hole with its snug parlour and well-stocked larder – of Doc's twisted grin, Alice's dark eyes, and the fact that Alfie would be there now, up in the attic.

'When Alfie's back on his feet he can help Doc until he's ready to go back into the field,' replied Aka. Even his voice was mysterious – low and terse.

'Field? What field?'

'Back into action – Alfie's been recruited into active service, and now I'm recruiting you. You'll obey orders without question, and your orders are to return to the farm. It's important to the Resistance that Honeysuckle Farm keeps going.'

'Why?'

Aka smiled. 'Flinty,' he said. 'Ask no questions, hear no lies. The farm's important to us for reasons that must remain secret. That's all you need to know.'

'I don't understand what's going on. I don't know how Tumbleweed and Doc and the bandits work together.'

'You don't know how the bits fit? Or who's in charge? Or why one patch of ground might be more important than another?'

'No.'

'Good. Just do your bit – forget about the other bits. That way you can't spill too many beans if you're captured. There's a chain of command – that's all you need to know – Lord Blade's at the top, and guess who is at the bottom?'

'Me?'

'Got it in one! Lord Razor Blade's at the top, you're at the bottom, and I'm somewhere in between.'

'What about Tumbleweed?'

'She comes and goes. She's a—' But before he could say anything more Aka grabbed Flint by a shoulder and tugged him towards the hedge. 'Spotter plane!' he hissed. 'Keep still.'

He didn't whisper – that would have been absurd. In his normal voice he explained that no one flying overhead, no matter how low, could identify a well-camouflaged bandit lying against a hedge unless he moved – and they were both well camouflaged.

The little plane skimmed overhead, then out over the

sea, where it disappeared into a threatening bank of low cloud, turned and reappeared, skimming back over the fields half a mile to the west.

'Keep your head down,' said Aka, 'until we can't see them or hear them. Then keep close to cover. They can spot you walking across a field from miles off.'

They watched the circling plane until the low clouds blew in from the sea and shrouded the fields with mist and drizzle. Aka led Flint stealthily from field to field, skirting the high hedges, until the boy began to recognise his surroundings.

'You know where you are now?'

'Yes – Green Meadow.'

'And you remember the way from here?'

'Yes.'

'Then off you go.'

Back in the Bolt Hole attic, Alfie was enjoying himself. He was propped up on two pillows, his right arm was firmly bandaged, and a dark-eyed girl was gazing at him.

'She wouldn't have wanted to put a proper, trained signaller into an exposed and vulnerable position,' Alfie was explaining to Alice. 'She wouldn't want to risk the life of anyone who was any use.' As you can see, Alfie was as much of a smart-arse as ever. 'This is why she chose Flinty,' he explained with a happy grin. (A generous shot of morphine tends to encourage happy grins even if you're wounded.)

Alice gazed at the teenage bandit with her wide, dark

eyes. Apparently he'd been specially trained to kill with his bare hands, although he preferred to use his Fairbairn fighting knife for close-quarter combat because, as he'd told her nonchalantly, 'they don't get a chance to scream!' She'd helped bandage the young hero's wounded hand and arm; now she was listening to his account of Benedict Dingle Flint's part in the day's action.

'Can I have the bullet?'

'What bullet?'

'The one Grandpa dug out of your hand with his tweezers.'

That was OK with Alfie: if you're a hero you have to put up with a little hero worship. 'Of course you can have it,' he laughed. 'What will you do with it?'

'I'll wear it round my neck.'

Alfie raised his bloody bandage to his right eyebrow and gave her a jaunty salute.

7

Old Kent was sowing kale. He might have been blind, and he might have lost all his farm hands, but he could still think. He'd worked out that he could feed his herd with forage crops so long as he sowed little and often. 'Little and often,' he'd told Ma.

'So you keep saying,' she'd replied. 'Little and often! Little and often!'

'That's right,' Old Kent had flashed her a smile with his perfect dentures. 'We don't have the labour to make much hay, or silage, or lift fodder beet. So what do we do?'

'Plant kale.'

'And how do we do it?'

'Little and often.'

He was bouncing gently on the seat of the seed drill, his sightless eyes pointing at Turpin's tail. Ma Kent had been recruited to waddle from one side of the field to the other in time to catch Turpin by the bridle and turn him. This is the thing about carthorses – they can see, hear and think. Turpin was able to pull the drill in roughly the right direction, and if he strayed wildly, a yelp from Ma would alert Old Kent to tug at the reins.

Ma Kent was not in a sunny mood. The mud clung to her boots, the drizzle ran down her sou'wester and trickled down her neck. Waddling in the rain was not Ma Kent's favourite pastime – she was more of an indoor waddler. She thought about her warm kitchen and the pastry she should have been making.

'That Alfie,' she muttered. 'He seems to think he can come and go as he pleases. And what about the other one – the little fellow who'd not say boo to a goose? What happened to him?'

'You know what happened to him,' cried Old Kent, who'd reached the hedge and needed turning. 'Same as happens to all of them that's rounded up. They're shot! That's what happened to Flinty. How old was he?'

'Twelve.'

'Twelve,' growled Old Kent. He went on to say exactly what he thought of shooting children, but he'd been pulled, lurched and rattled out of Ma's earshot. She watched him talking indignantly to the horse's tail and shook her cold, wet head. Then she turned at a noise behind her and cried out in surprise.

Jock the Border Collie was prancing and dancing around the ghostly form of Benedict Dingle Flint.

The unfortunate child had apparently returned from the dead. His face was green, and he had some sort of woollen bonnet rammed over his head, decorated with grass and twigs.

'You!' she whimpered.

'Yes,' was the reply.

'You've come back!' she sobbed.

'I've been sent.'

'Why did they send *you*?' she wailed. 'They should have sent my Brian!'

Ma Kent lifted her wet face in the direction of heaven as if she was thinking of making a complaint. There were tears on her cheeks as well as drizzle. Suddenly she was running, or at least waddling at speed; full of anger and tears, she was heading for the ruined farmhouse and her snug kitchen.

This is why, when Turpin next needed turning, it was Flint that caught him by the bridle. The great horse stopped to allow himself to have his soft nose stroked and his neck patted. Old Kent sensed someone new was on the scene.

'It's me,' said Flint faintly. Ma Kent's reaction had shocked him. For the first time ever he felt sorry for her.

The farmer recognised the boy's voice but, because he could not see his light green face, he did not jump to any supernatural conclusion. 'What happened?' he asked.

He meant what happened after Flint had been arrested, but the boy assumed he was talking about the ambush, so he replied, 'I'm not allowed to say.'

Kent nodded.

'But Alfie's wounded,' he told the farmer. 'I'm to stop here to help.'

'Alfie's mixed up with the Resistance,' sighed Old Kent, 'like my son was.'

'Brian?'

Old Kent turned his ruined face towards Flint. 'We never saw him for months after the Germans landed,' he sighed. 'Then one night I was out in the yard – Alfie was there with me – and a voice calls out, "Hello Dad," and it was him. "You never saw me," he said. "No," I said, "I'm blind." Then he slaps me on the back. "Don't tell Mum," he says. "She'll blab."

'And that's the last I ever saw of him. I don't think he realised I'd really gone blind – just thought I was playing along with him. Then a couple of weeks later an envelope came through the letterbox in the middle of the night, and inside was a note saying *We regret to inform you that your son Brian has been killed in action.* Didn't say where or when, or what he'd been doing, or if they'd buried him or just left him in a ditch. Don't you join the Resistance, Flinty, just because Alfie has. You're not cut out for it.'

'No,' agreed Benedict Dingle Flint. 'I expect you're right.'

'Someone's got to do the milking,' said Old Kent kindly. 'Or all the heroes would starve.'

Wise words – but a little too late.

Dr Six was at Camp Vigilant. He'd got wet running from the airstrip into the castle. He took off his dripping leather coat and handed it to a junior officer before striding to the fire to warm himself. He accepted a mug of hot coffee and turned until his back was to the glowing coals and he was facing the Gestapo man holding his coat.

'What are they saying about the death of Queen Wallis?' he asked him.

'People are saying it seems a bit fishy.'

'Fishy?'

'Yes – SOE specialise in accidents.'

'They certainly do. And the Resistance around these parts has been particularly active lately. There was that ambush the other day.'

'And there was the roadside bomb.'

'Time for reprisals – *significant* reprisals!'

'Significant?'

'A hundred – and include children!' Dr Six did not want the world to know that the British had almost certainly succeeded in assassinating the puppet queen, but he wanted Newfoundland to guess that he'd guessed. A reprisal of that magnitude would tell them.

'Children?'

'Particularly boys!'

*

It had been some time since the legendary Firebrand Flint had starred in any of Benedict's daydreams. Of course, he was still a dreamer, but recently the dreams had been about what he called the *Happy Days*. He was daydreaming about those old days as he unhitched Turpin, watched him clatter and clop to the trough, and went to make sure there was hay in his manger.

Mr Flint, of Hornbeams, Willow Way, was a cheery chap with a face like the Mad Hatter's, only without the top hat. His dark hair, receding gracefully, had been burnished with Brylcreem until it gleamed. His glasses had been polished, his suit had been brushed, and his spirits had recently been fortified by two Eccles cakes and a cup of tea. ''Twas brillig,' he informed his wife, 'and the slithy toves did gyre and gimble in the wabe.'

'What's a tove?' asked Benedict. His dad brushed this absurd question aside, lifted his little son onto the top of the coffee table and continued talking nonsense:

'"And hast thou slain the Jabberwock?
Come to my arms, my beamish boy!
O frabjous day! Callooh! Callay!"
He chortled in his joy.'

Mr Flint bowed to his wife; he bowed to his son. Then he proceeded to give an instructive example of frabjous joy by doing the Hokey Cokey.

Back in the yard at Honeysuckle Farm Flint was singing along with his daydream:

'"You put your left leg in,
Your left leg out,

In, out, in, out,

You shake it all about . . ."

Left legs in, Turpin! Left legs out!'

Turpin was above such frivolity. His legs remained firmly in place, and so did those of Jock the Border Collie – but they were both impressed.

It was good, now that Alfie was gone, that Flint still had two firm friends.

The Type 28 anti-tank pillbox had not been built for comfort. The wind blew in from the sea, sang through its gaping windows and wailed out of the canvas door. Alfie had made special shutters for the windows that faced the sea. He'd skilfully hacked and battered them out of corrugated iron to form crude windbreaks. Flint remembered how proud Alfie had been when he'd first bashed them into place. It felt strange being alone as he jammed the crude shutters into the windows until the breeze no longer wailed but whistled – a soothing sound.

Alfie had also invented a weird chimney; he'd constructed it from chicken wire and cement. When the nights were cold, a cheerful driftwood fire always smouldered in an old oil drum that had been hacked full of holes with an axe. The wood would burn, the smoke would rise, and the weird chimney would guide 69 per cent of it out of a window.

Flint looked at the hot, smoking drum and wondered how serious Alfie's wound was. Would he lose an arm? If so, he'd be a one-armed bandit! Flint smiled. *He'll be OK,* he told himself. *Alfie's probably immortal! He's most probably got special lizard-like powers and can grow new limbs.*

These thoughts were comforting, like his dreams. He took off his boots, snuggled under the rugs, and turned up his oil lamp. With his head resting on Jock's ribs, Flint began to read: *It was the first day of the Christmas holidays, and William had spent a happy morning roaming the countryside.* Jock stirred. He began to growl – a low threatening sound. Flint rolled towards the door and pulled back the flap.

Headlights were approaching.

8

Flint remembered the last time headlights had swept up the drive. He leapt out of his bed and darted into the yard with Jock at his heels. By the time they'd made it to Turpin's stable, the truck had halted and soldiers were jumping to the ground. The headlights still blazed, so he could see them clearly as they kicked the door in.

'Don't bark! Please don't bark!' whispered Flint. He shrank back into the shadows and peered over the stable door.

A shot echoed from the ruined farmhouse. Old Kent must have got to the shotgun he kept under his bed; he'd kept it there since the last time the Nazis had called. There were answering shots – the chatter of automatic rifles – then an eerie silence until Ma Kent was bundled out of the house in her winceyette nightdress.

She was screaming.

Dawn arrived from over the sea – stirring the seagulls and waking the cockerel. The truck had gone. Flint pushed open the stable door and emerged cautiously into the farmyard. He approached the silent house but did not dare to enter it. *I should go in,* he told himself. *He might be still alive.* Jock whined. The boy stood motionless; to his left pigs snuffled and grunted; to his right the ruined farmhouse stood silent. Flint did not move. Jock licked his fingers. They waited.

There was an unexpectedly cheery shout.

'Flinty!' yelled Alfie, bounding briskly across the yard. He grabbed Flint's hand and shook it vigorously; for a second or two there was some slight danger that Flint's arm might be wrenched from its socket, but luckily Alfie dropped the hand so he could slap Flint's back as if he was beating a drum. Alfie was dancing now – prancing about. He bounced in like a fairground boxer and punched Flint playfully on his shoulder. He capered around him. He seemed about to burst. He held up his right hand.

'Look!' he cried. 'What do you think of that?'

'You've lost your fingers!'

'Not all of them. I've still got my thumb – and my trigger finger – and my arm's OK, thanks to Doc's maggots.

I'm fighting fit, Flinty – fighting fit. But how are you, my old dung-shifter? Sharp as ever?' He exploded with laughter. 'I've been sent to see if all is well. Is all well, Flinty my old chum? Is everything tickety-boo?'

Flint shook his head.

'You think he's been shot?' asked Alfie when Flint had told him what he guessed had happened. Flint nodded.

'I suppose we should go and see,' said Alfie doubtfully. He turned and took a hesitant step towards the farmhouse. 'Are you coming?' he asked. 'I don't want to go in by myself.'

Flint nodded; he could hardly refuse.

As night fell, Old Kent's body, wrapped in sacking and weighted down with rocks, was slid into the sea off Flat Rock.

'Do you think we should say something?' asked Flint as he watched the bubbles.

'Goodbye, old fellow,' said Alfie, rising to the occasion as if he'd been a bishop of the Church of England. 'You ploughed a straight furrow.'

'Amen,' sobbed Benedict Dingle Flint.

'What shall we do now?' asked Flint.

'Aka will know what to do.'

'You're going back?'

'I have to obey orders,' said Alfie. 'I was sent to check up on Honeysuckle Farm and report back – but before I go I'll help you clean up.'

'Thanks.'

'Don't worry, Flinty. Aka won't leave you here all by yourself. You're not – not worried about ghosts, are you?'

'Not until now,' squeaked Flint anxiously. 'Not until you put the idea into my head. Thank you very much, Alfie, very thoughtful of you.' He did his best to smile, but did not quite succeed.

'It'd be nice to see Old Kent again,' suggested Alfie thoughtfully. 'Except there's no such thing as ghosts,' he added quickly, 'so you'll be denied that pleasure.'

'It's easy not to believe in ghosts when it's daylight,' replied Flint. 'It'll be harder when it's dark, and the wind's whistling through the windows, and a rat goes scuttling past.'

'If Jock growls it'll be a rat. If he whines it'll be a ghost.'

'A ghost that doesn't exist?'

'I wish they did,' sighed Alfie. 'I wish my dad and your dad were ghosts. I wish they'd call round every now and then for a chat. I wish Old Kent was a ghost too. But they're not, Flinty, they're dead and gone.'

'You'll come back soon, won't you, Alfie?'

'Trust me!' said Alfie, giving a thumbs-up with his lonely right thumb. 'We're a team.' And he clapped Flint on both shoulders.

Three nights later Jock growled. Flint woke in the dark and listened. These were not ghosts – not unless ghosts could drive. The boy hushed the dog and slid out from under his rugs. It was that time of night when the

Gestapo called, and if it was them he wanted to be as far away as it was possible to run.

Voices! He could hear voices.

'Hullo!' one of them cried in English. It was a woman's voice. 'Benedict?' it called. 'Where are you?'

Flint slipped out of the pillbox and went to investigate.

Doc Bolt's Trojan was parked in front of the farmhouse and the old fellow was busy unloading boxes from the back. 'Radio equipment,' he greeted Flint, slapping him on the back and ruffling his hair. 'Secret Sweeties,' he explained, pointing at the two women in slacks and waterproof jackets waiting by the door. One was tall, the other small and wearing specs. They smiled at the boy in the light of the headlights.

'I suppose you thought "Secret Sweeties" would be young and beautiful,' one of them laughed. 'Not old bags.'

'Don't worry, Flinty,' laughed Doc. 'They're quite nice old bags.'

'I was young and beautiful when I was recruited,' explained the tall one. 'Cicely was just young.'

'It was a long time ago, Benedict,' said the one with the specs, 'quite a different war.'

'The Great War?' asked Flint politely.

'For me, yes, but with Flossie it was much, much earlier.'

'The Hundred Years' War?' asked Flint, raising his right eyebrow.

Cicely laughed. 'Yes – although, to be fair, she didn't start till halfway through. Be a love, Benedict, and show us where the kettle is; we've just parachuted in from darkest Newfoundland and we will DIE if we don't have a cup of tea. And by the way, we have some news for you.'

'News?' asked Flint.

'About your mum.'

9

'**O**ur friends in the army have been unhelpful,' Dr Six told his Death Squad chiefs. There were forty of them – or thirty-nine and a half if you counted the wounded Vogler, who had just crept into the meeting with the aid of an ebony-handled walking stick. He was thinner, paler, and walked with a limp, but his deeply impressive walrus moustache was as luxurious as ever. (He'd taken to brushing it with a baby's hairbrush to make it gleam and shine.)

They were in the orangery at Kensington Palace – a long room with a long table with Dr Six on his feet with the spring sun shining through the windows and lighting up his ears. He paused in his speech to give the wounded man time to ease himself into a chair and prop the walking stick against the table. Vogler's eyes twinkled as he acknowledged the murmur of good wishes from the assembled torturers and thugs. If he was in pain he did not show it. If he was exhausted, no one could tell.

It was important not to show weakness or spend too much time in a hospital bed. It wasn't just the enemy that had to be outwitted, it was the other Death Squad chiefs. Vogler knew Dr Six had been making plans to replace him on the grounds that he was too sick to be useful. That's why he'd turned up – to show everyone he was still in the game, even if he was pale, frail and smelling of hospital.

Dr Six cleared his throat and started again. The forty Gestapo men gazed at their chief with a mixture of fear, admiration and scorn. All of them were wary of him; they knew he'd saved Hitler's life that December day in Trafalgar Square, and that the good doctor had the authority to execute members of his own staff if he thought they were slacking. It was a power he exercised at regular intervals; he liked his chiefs to know that any blunder could be fatal. Despite this, half of them thought he was a genius. The other half believed he was mad – particularly Vogler. He should be replaced by Count Kasimir von dem Wappenbuch – that was Vogler's opinion. The count was a natural leader.

He glanced sideways and caught the count's eye. He winked to remind him that they both agreed Dr Six was a liability who should be put down like a mad dog. Von dem Wappenbuch was six foot two, rugged and handsome. They'd given him *three* Iron Crosses back in the Great War, and the scar on his high right cheek was absolutely genuine – etched into the bone by the same twisted metal flange that had also skewered out his left eye the day he'd been shot down – 4 February 1918. He turned in Vogler's direction and, instead of winking back, tapped his glass eye with the end of his golden fountain pen.

'The fact is, gentlemen,' thundered Dr Six, 'until Russia is defeated we will never have enough troops to hold this island. Take a look at this.' He turned and snapped his fingers. A female auxiliary in the uniform of the SS-Helferin appeared from a side room pushing what looked to Vogler like a hospital trolley. Lying on it was the dead body of a soldier in battledress.

Dr Six waited. He brandished his swagger stick at the corpse. 'Yesterday our air base on the Lizard was attacked,' he informed them tensely. 'Aircraft were destroyed, fuel and ammunition dumps blown up, aircrew murdered, and the entire garrison wiped out, but there were some enemy losses. This man is one of them. Observe the boots, gentlemen.'

Eighty eyes (one of them made of glass) focussed on the dead man's boots.

'These boots were manufactured by the Alberta Boot Company.' Dr Six paused to let the grim significance sink in. 'This man is not a local bandit. Look at the badge on his shoulder. This soldier is an Australian commando wearing Canadian boots. There were no Australian divisions in this island at the time of the invasion – only British and Canadian. The Australians were in North Africa. So how, exactly, was the Lizard air base attacked last night by Australians?'

'They come in from Newfoundland,' sighed the count, with a weary shake of his head, 'wearing brand-new boots!'

'Yes!' agreed the chief of chiefs, 'and look at this map. Look at the south-west peninsula.' He pointed with his swagger stick. 'It juts out into the Atlantic – it is riddled with secluded coves. Units from Newfoundland can be landed on any dark night. What we're up against is the most effective network of resistance fighters in occupied Europe fighting alongside elite forces, based overseas, who can come and go at will. And we do not have the manpower to tackle them. What we *can* do – and what I intend to do – in the south-west is to scorch bandit country. Destroy every building. Burn every haystack. Shoot every domestic animal and round up every civilian under the age of ninety-three. I shall create a desert from sea to sea!

'Any questions?'

'Tell me again,' Flint cried, jumping up from behind the kitchen table.

Cicely laughed. She'd told him the good news three times already, but it was such fun telling the kid that his long-lost mother was alive that she didn't mind doing it again. She took a sip of tea.

'Well,' she said, 'it was just after Christmas the year of the invasion, and I was based up north. Anyway, our lads derailed this heavily guarded train. It was probably bound for West Yorkshire, where the Germans were setting up concentration camps, because it was full of political prisoners and criminals.' She nibbled some cake. 'We had to interview the survivors.'

'To see if they were criminals or political prisoners?'

'Yes. That's when I met your mum. I can remember her because everyone was talking about the Trafalgar Square thing – about the famous Dingle Flint and how he'd nearly shot Hitler – so as soon as she told me her name I knew she was a political straight away. Besides, criminals don't wear fitted skirts – or cry quite so much.'

Flint blinked back his own tears and waited for Cicely to continue.

'She was in a bit of a state,' she went on, 'which is what you'd expect if your husband's just been executed and you've been grilled by the Gestapo. Anyway, I interviewed her to see whether or not she was a gangster, and, after weighing up the evidence for about half a second, I formed the opinion that she wasn't, so I showed her the door and said, "Next!" – and that's the last I saw of her.'

'But she's alive?'

'Alive and kicking. They'll have taken her to Scotland – the Nazis hadn't occupied it at that stage of the war –

and from there she'd have probably been flown to Newfoundland!'

Life at Honeysuckle Farm was much improved by the arrival of the two Sweeties. They bustled, laughed and sang. They cooked roast dinners, pies and full English breakfasts. Their SOE spy radio had been hidden in the back kitchen, under the milk skimmer.

Every day, after an encouraging breakfast, Benedict Dingle Flint – watched alertly by Jock the Border Collie – hitched up Turpin. To the casual eye – and the casual nose – the noble horse looked (and smelt) as if he was pulling a cart full of dung. But the manure at the top was in fact only a foot deep; the cart had been skilfully converted into a small mobile cell and fitted with a transmitter. Flint had to charge the battery every so often – which he did with the tractor – but otherwise the unit was simple to operate.

Flint liked to keep the manure fresh; it was more realistic that way. For this reason, the first thing he did after hitching Turpin up was to drive him round to the muck pile, fork off yesterday's dung, and replace it with another layer – warm, soft and steaming. No Gestapo goon would for one instant suspect that a covert radio out-station was hidden under that layer of muck.

Once the fresh manure was in place, Flint drove the secret unit to an agreed destination – usually a field a couple of miles away from Honeysuckle Farm. Once there, he unhitched Turpin and ran out the aerial for fifty feet before securing it to a tree. That's how the system worked: there'd always be one Sweetie listening in on the spy radio under the milk skimmer. Every so often Aka called in with a message to transmit, and a Sweetie would climb onto her bike, pedal furiously to the appointed field, clamber into the abandoned cart, and there – under a shield of manure – send the coded message on its way to distant Newfoundland.

Flint just set things up and took things back again. For most of the day he was back on the farm collecting eggs, feeding pigs, milking cows, planting kale, and dreaming dreams. Every day the milk lorry collected the churns from Honeysuckle Farm, and, once a month, the Milk Board sent a cheque. Flint took that cheque to Old Kent's bank and paid it into the Honeysuckle Farm account. Then the Secret Sweeties, who had been trained in forgery, paid the bills using Old Kent's cheque book. Perfect! One early evening Flint was up on Green Meadow, the time of day he liked to devote to ferreting – not to mention dreaming:

The beautiful Lady Tumbleweed was drawn to Firebrand Flint like a moth to a flame. It was partly the young fighter ace's devil-may-care smile, and partly his ability to squawk like Daffy Duck.

'Champagne, my lady?' croaked Alfie, his faithful butler, offering her a silver tray. 'Or Lucozade if you'd prefer. Hey!' he suddenly yelled. 'Flinty, you mad, daydreaming freak!'

Flint abandoned his Lady Tumbleweed dream, and turned to face the grinning, bouncing figure of the real Alfie, who was bounding towards him.

10

'**T**wo boys required, Flinty old son, for a secret mission.' Alfie tapped his nose. 'Top secret – my lips are sealed – don't ask me about it. Careless talk costs lives! But there is nothing secret about this.' He thrust a strange instrument into Flint's hands.

'What is it?'

'It's a present!' laughed Alfie. 'Doc found it in the cellar of the Imperial Hotel.'

'Yes, but what is it?'

'A ukulele, of course! Alice wants you to master it. The sweet young thing wants to hear you twanging it under her window like a little Romeo. She's busy knitting.'

'Knitting?'

'Knitting the tights!'

Flint laughed. He realised just how much he'd missed Alfie.

'A secret mission?' he asked anxiously as they made their way back to the farm.

'You worry too much,' said Alfie, glancing at his watch. They'd given him a special watch – the sort you check alertly when they say, *'Synchronise watches!'*

Flint could see smoke curling from the farmhouse chimney into the evening air. Swallows – or possibly swifts – skimmed past. Beyond Three Corner Field the sea lay calm.

'You're frightened of dying, that's the trouble,' Alfie continued.

Flint's eyes opened wide. He just couldn't believe what Alfie was saying; in Flint's book anyone who wasn't frightened of dying was raving mad.

'But everyone dies, Flinty, sooner or later.'

'I'd sooner it was later – as late as possible.'

'Not really an option.' Alfie was serious for once. 'What choice is there? I'll tell you – you can be shipped to Germany when you're seventeen, where they'll *work* you to death. Or you can choose to die young and take some of the bastards with you. Your dad was a hero, Flinty. He'll be up in heaven watching the turn of events – are you going to let the old chap down?'

'No,' sighed Flint. 'It's just that . . .'

'You're not the heroic type?'

'No.'

'They're going to kill you,' Alfie announced cheerfully. 'It could be tomorrow – or it could be years ahead. But it's going to happen, so go after them while you can and keep smiling. You can do that, can't you? You can keep smiling?'

'Yes.'

'Now you're fully equipped with a ukulele, you can keep everyone smiling.'

This was true. Flint arched his eyebrows and squiffled up his hair until it stood on end. He turned to Alfie, nodded, and agreed with him using a special voice – a cross between his Stan Laurel impression and Bugs Bunny with a sore throat. 'Yes,' he squawked, nodding his head some more. 'That'll be my contribution to the war effort!'

He twanged the uke.

It was rabbit pie for supper – with a bay leaf and a china blackbird – everything right and proper, as you'd expect from an old bag.

'She used to make pies for Charles Dickens,' joked Cicely. 'She was famous for it – veal and ham pies – they called her the cat snatcher.'

'Don't pay any attention,' advised Flossie. 'She's been at the cooking sherry again. I might have to send a dispatch to Lord Blade. He'll probably want her shot.'

'Who exactly *is* Lord Blade?' asked Flint, through a mouthful of pie crust.

'Good question,' cried Alfie, who was tucking in eagerly.

'Royal Flying Corps,' said Cicely. 'In the last war – a lot of our aces were Canadian – because, obviously, they're all crack shots.'

'On account of the bears,' explained Flossie.

'He was one of them,' continued Cicely. 'Born in a log cabin in the frozen north.' She paused to fork a forkful of pie into her mouth. 'He was in the government – Churchill's government, that's why he's a lord – and when all was lost the old man sent him to Newfoundland with Princess Elizabeth. His orders were to wage war by fair means or foul!'

'Now he's in charge,' Alfie chipped in. 'Because Churchill and the rest of them are all dead.'

'That's right,' agreed Flossie. 'In charge of what's left of the army, the navy and the air force – in charge of all the spies – in charge of the Resistance – every unit, every Secret Sweetie – in charge of me and in charge of you.'

'Fair means or foul, Flinty,' grinned Alfie. 'Are you up for that?'

Alfie had always been full of fizz and extra whizz – but now he'd been sworn into the Resistance and had lost three fingers to prove it, he simply buzzed and bounced with energy.

'I took the oath,' he kept telling Flint, as soon as the two boys were alone in their pillbox. 'I was sworn in. I'm a soldier. I've got a rank and number.'

'Rank?' asked Flint. 'What are you then? A general?'

'Not yet.' Alfie capered round the Type 28. It was like watching Tigger. It was like sharing the pillbox with a giant talking puppy.

'So?' asked Flint. 'If you've been recruited what are you doing swanning about here?'

'I'm sorry, my dear old twanger of the uke, but for a moment there I thought I heard you say, "swanning about".' Alfie sighed and shook his tousled head in disbelief.

'Aren't you supposed to go out every night causing havoc?'

'I'm here under orders, Flinty.'

'Secret orders?'

'Of course!'

'So they ordered you to come back to Honeysuckle Farm. Isn't that like ordering you to stay out of their way?'

Alfie gazed at Flint with an air of infinite patience. 'Didn't I tell you we're being sent on a mission?' he said. 'Two boys, that's what's they've asked for – I'm one of them and you're the other.' He smiled a crafty smile and tapped his nose.

'What mission?' asked Flint warily, but Alfie was no longer listening. He was gazing out of a window at the sea. 'What's that?' he gasped, pointing at a mysterious vessel nosing past Honeysuckle Cove.

'The patrol boat.'

'What patrol boat? She's flying the swastika!'

'It's one of theirs. She's been coming past every day –

up and down the coast. And I've even seen her at night, without lights.'

Alfie scratched his head with what was left of his right hand. 'Wow!' he hissed. 'That's thrown a spanner in the works! I suppose I'll have to tell you now: our mission, Flinty, is to escort a little team of ruffians upcountry – a little team of ruffians that will be landing at Honeysuckle Cove tomorrow night. Well, they won't be able to land with that thing nosing about!' He pointed at the patrol boat. 'We have to report this,' he said. 'Let's get the Sweeties on the case!'

That night a coded message went out from the aerial in the covert cart. Flint was standing near, ready to drive it back to the farm; he was listening to Turpin scrunching up mouthfuls of grass and thinking about the mystery of radio. He didn't really understand how it worked, but he did know that the secret message would be relayed from station to station – from a field three miles north of Honeysuckle Farm to one of the Northern Isles which the Germans had failed to conquer, and from there to Iceland, Greenland, and finally Newfoundland.

Six minutes and thirty-five seconds later a radio message crackled through Flossie's earphones: Lord Blade wanted the patrol boat sunk.

Operation Sleep with the Fishes had started!

11

Doc arrived in the middle of the night with new orders: the boys were to report to the Bolt Hole the next morning with the little grey tractor and a load of hay.

They arrived to find the Bolt Hole humming with activity. Flint recognised some of the men who had taken part in the ambush – the TCM as Alfie called it.

'TCM?' Flint had asked.

'Tea-Cosy Massacre!'

The bandits were busy in the yard, bustling cheerfully about and cracking jokes with Doc, being watched from over the top of the latest Famous Five book by Alice, who was sitting comfortably in a deck chair enjoying the sunshine.

'Tumbleweed arrived last night,' she told the boys. 'She's still in bed catching up on her beauty sleep. She parachuted in. She doesn't like parachuting in case she twists her ankle – besides,' she continued earnestly, 'it can't be very elegant jumping out of an aeroplane in a skirt. She brought me this,' she said, holding up a new book. '*Five at Dead Man's Creek*.'

She gave Flint a friendly smile, because she knew he was a bit of a bookworm like herself and had read all the William books. Then she turned to give Alfie an even friendlier smile, because he could drive a tractor. There was no mention of the ukulele, and she was certainly not knitting any tights.

Flint was a tiny bit jealous – especially when a troop of bandits in Tommy Atkins helmets and submachine guns slung across their shoulders came slinking in from the woods to greet Alfie by ruffling his hair, slapping his back, and making friendly insults about his maimed hand. 'You should get a hook,' one of them suggested. 'That way you'd find it easier to wipe your . . .' He caught sight of the girl in the deckchair and stopped.

'Nose?' asked Alice.

'Eyes,' replied the bandit.

'This is the legendary Benedict Dingle Flint!' announced Alfie to the bandits.

They grinned and nodded. 'Where's your tea cosy?' they wanted to know.

He noticed Alice peeping at him from over the top of her book as if she thought he was a bit of a daredevil.

'The son of the famous Dingle Flint!' proclaimed Alfie to a roar of approval. Alice stopped reading for several seconds. Flint didn't quite morph into Firebrand mode, but he did give her a wink.

Bandits didn't like working in daylight, so there was a lot of grumbling and mumbling. Mostly they grumbled about naval intelligence. According to Doc Bolt, naval intelligence was a contradiction in terms. 'Sinking a ship,' he muttered, 'on a sunny day. We're bandits – we're nocturnal, like owls!'

Alfie remained sitting comfortably on the tractor seat, pretending his shortage of fingers made it impossible for him to help load the trailer. This was smart thinking, because the canisters of high explosive were heavy, and lugging them up from the Bolt Hole cellar was back-breaking work. Flint busied himself at the back of the trailer heaping hay over the canisters.

'That's the ticket,' growled the patrol's bomb maker – a broad-shouldered, flat-faced youth known as the Master Blaster. 'Keep them well out of sight and make sure there's room for the raft.'

'What raft?'

'It's going to be a floating booby trap disguised as a life raft,' explained the Blaster with a cunning smile. 'And here comes the corpse!'

A van skidded into the Bolt Hole yard. Aka jumped down from the driver's side, and a wild-looking youth jumped out from the other. 'That's Bugs,' said Alfie. 'Bugs the Rat Catcher.'

The new arrivals opened the back of their van and pulled out a dead body.

'Bait,' explained the Master Blaster. 'Show a crew of German sailors a dead Hun on a life raft and they'll go in to fish him out of it. And as soon as they move him –BANG!'

Flint watched in horror as the body was carried to the end of his trailer and dumped over the tailboard.

'Cover him with hay!' instructed Aka. 'Now, Flint, I'm swearing you in. That will mean that if you're killed in action, your wife will get a widow's pension – just as soon as we win the war. Are you married?'

'No.'

'Well, you won't cost any more than the little white cross, then. Now, repeat after me: "I, Benedict Dingle Flint . . ."'

'"I, Benedict Dingle Flint,"' Flint repeated after Aka, '"swear by Almighty God that I will be faithful and bear true allegiance to Her Majesty Queen Elizabeth the Second, and will observe and obey all orders of the generals and officers set over me. So help me God."'

'That's me,' growled Aka.

'What?'

'I'm the officer set over you – that's why you'll need God's help! Now jump down and take a look at the raft the Crab Catchers are building.' He nodded in the direction of the old sables. 'We call them Crab Catchers because they're fishermen's sons. Go and see what they're doing.'

'It's got to look like a life raft,' one of the three Crab Catchers explained to Flint when he and Aka arrived in the old stable.

'But it's a little boat!'

'Easy to move into position,' explained Aka, 'and fill with marzipan.' He was talking about plastic explosive, which smelt like marzipan. 'She'll look like a life raft by the time we've finished with her. She'll be heavy in the water – what with the dead body and the bomb – too heavy to take a man at the oars. This is where you come in, Flinty, you being as light as a paper bag full of eiderdown. You can row, can't you?'

Flint felt the blood draining from his extremities as he cottoned on that he'd be rowing a floating bomb, and when he answered his voice was faint and his throat was dry. 'Yes,' he managed to reply. 'We used to live near the river. We had a Thames skiff. Dad taught me to row.'

'Can you swim?' asked a Crab Catcher with a harpoon tattoo. 'Because you'll have to take her out a long way and swim back.'

Flint nodded. He was trying to seem confident and brave – trying to stop his hands trembling. 'Yes,' he gulped. 'I can swim.'

After a brisk brunch of bread and bacon the bandits were ready. The Crab Catchers lugged the raft to the trailer, where Alfie and Flint covered it with hay.

'Just sit on top,' instructed Alfie, 'to stop it blowing

about. And don't look so worried – relax! Have you brought your ukulele?'

'No, for some strange reason I thought we could manage without it.'

'That's the spirit, Flinty – nonchalant and cool – get that eyebrow working – that's it! Your dad will be proud of you!' Alfie believed dead dads watched from above, with critical interest and high expectations.

The Gestapo certainly watched from the sky; the boys had only driven a mile or so towards the sea when a spotter plane dived low over the tractor. Alfie waved – he always gave a friendly wave when Jerry flew over. Back in the trailer Flint pretended to be asleep. *There's enough high explosive under this hay to sink a battleship!* he thought anxiously as the little plane circled overhead. *Boxes of the stuff – not to mention the boat and the dead body dressed as a sailor!* But what could have looked more innocent than a couple of farm boys with a load of hay? To Flint's relief the plane headed west; he sat up and looked round. They were driving through farmland now. The fields were unfamiliar; Aka had decided that the patrol boat was to be sunk off a rocky headland eight miles west of Honeysuckle Cove.

To Flint's surprise there was no track leading to the shore – just a sheer cliff face, no path and no beach. Aka had picked the most dangerous, desolate, remote and inaccessible place he knew – but at least there was cover. Stunted trees, scrub, thorn and brambles fringed the cliff top. The bandits were already there – hidden and waiting impatiently. They'd been taken most of the way by road in the back of Doc's Trojan, and now they were growling at the boys, blaming them for taking too long. Alfie was grinning back at them, tapping the side of his head to suggest they were raving loons, and gently pointing out that a certain amount of caution was required when one was towing a trailer stuffed with Explosive 808.

'Get the stiff out first,' Aka ordered curtly. One of the fishermen's sons lashed the rope's end round the dead man's ankles, no doubt using a fishermen's bend. The Master Blaster and Bugs the Rat Catcher were waiting expectantly on the rocks below; they stowed the corpse in the mouth of a cave and looked up for the next offering from above. The 'life raft' was soon sliding down the cliff towards them.

Soon the three young fishermen and the Master Blaster were making their final preparations.

Aka turned to the watching boys. 'If they were soldiers they'd smell a rat,' he explained. 'Soldiers are used to booby traps – especially in occupied territory – and they know that baiting a trap with an enemy body is standard bandit practice. But these ones won't be soldiers – they'll be sailors, and the last thing they'll be expecting at sea is a booby trap.'

'It's important you do things right,' the Master Blaster was telling Flint. 'The best way you're going to remember is if I tell you what's going to happen – OK?'

Flint nodded apprehensively.

'Why can't I do it?' asked Alfie. He could tell Flint was scared.

'Because you're too heavy,' explained the one with the dolphin tattoo. 'Flint's just the right weight, and he can row. Can *you* row, Alfie?'

'It looks easy enough.'

'No, it's not,' snapped Aka, 'so stop playing the hero and obey orders. Get back up that cliff and drive the tractor and its trailer back to Honeysuckle Farm. We don't want it standing in the middle of the field drawing attention to itself.'

With one last anxious look at Flint, Alfie tore himself away and scrambled back up the cliff to obey orders.

'She's a little pram dinghy,' the one with the dolphin tattoo told Flint, 'but from the deck of a ship she'll look like a life raft.'

'Because of these,' said the one with the harpoon tattoo. He tapped at an empty oil drum. They had lashed drums all round the boat, and these, together with the tarpaulin, were designed to make the little craft look like a raft from above – the sort of life raft you'd make for if your ship had been torpedoed.

'Right,' continued the Master Blaster. 'Imagine you're aboard the patrol boat. What do you see bobbing in the waves?'

'A German sailor lying on a raft.'

'Right. So you give the alarm, and the captain gives the order, and you come alongside and over the side you go, and there's poor old Fritz looking stiff, so you grab the poor fellow round the shoulders so as to heave him up to your mates. And that's when the bomb goes off, because lifting the body will tug out the release switch on the detonator.'

'It's got to look like it's drifting,' said the one with the harpoon tattoo. 'That's why the anchor rope's been tucked under the forward barrel. When you chuck it overboard it won't be seen – not from above. That's all you've got to do, Flinty. Row her out until we wave at you; then over goes the anchor and you swim back. But for God's sake don't touch the body or you'll be blown to . . .'

'Smithereens?'

'Very tiny smithereens.'

They pushed him out into the sea. It was mid-afternoon by now and the wind had been rising. Waves thumped into the prow and banged the oil drum that had been lashed there. With his back to the horizon Flint was facing the dead body. He tried to look beyond it to where the bandits were standing up to their waists in sea water, watching him. The corpse was propped up in the stern. His eyes were wide open; blood had stained the white jersey.

Thump – thump – thump – the little boat bounced boldly into each succeeding wave, and, at each shock, the corpse shook. *If he slides over,* Flint thought grimly, *there'll be one hell of a bang! Try not to think about it. Just keep on rowing – it's not like the Thames, though, is it? That's not Mum sitting in the back opening her picnic hamper. Dad's not here saying, 'O frabjous day! Callooh!*

Callay!' and chortling in his joy. Mark you, thought Flint, *I am gyring and gimbling in the wabe – in fact there's rather too much gyring and gimbling, in my opinion. How much further do they want me to go? I'm miles out!*

But of course they wanted him far out into deep water – far enough out for the patrol boat to come alongside. She was really a small ship, so she wouldn't do that if there was the remotest chance of hitting a rock. Flint had rowed his grim little craft the best part of half a mile out before he was given the signal to drop anchor. By now, bigger waves were rolling in; perhaps the tide had turned. The boat crashed into each trough as he struggled with the anchor. At last he slipped over the side into the heaving deep.

He trod water and swallowed a salty mouthful. He thought of Old Kent. He thought of conger eels. Above him the floating bomb rose and fell, tugging at the anchor chain. He looked up, half expecting to see the pale face of the dead man leaning over the side to curse him.

When Flint turned towards the land the rocky shore seemed a mile away. Up he went as each wave rolled in, and then down, deep down, until the land was out of sight.

That's when the spotter plane returned. He heard its engines.

They mustn't see me, he thought. *They mustn't see my head!*

He sank beneath the surface and swam for the anchor rope. Then, with the rope in his hand, he resurfaced underneath the dinghy's prow and the overhanging oil drum. The plane circled overhead.

They'll be radioing their base, Flint reckoned. *That's good – they'll notify the patrol boat!*

At length the spotter flew on. Flint waited until he could no longer hear it – and it was then, just as he was about to break from cover, that he heard the distant throb of a marine engine.

The patrol boat had turned up, and Flint was still clinging on to the floating bomb!

12

hey heard the explosion at Honeysuckle Farm – almost eight miles away. Turpin pricked up his ears; Jock whined; the two Sweeties looked up from their radio. Alfie heard it as he bucketed down a lane on the tractor with the trailer bouncing behind him. The bandits heard it as they lay face down among the rocks. The shock wave passed over their heads; spray and shrapnel soared over them, and a towering wave raced to the shore, bringing with it the coughing, spluttering figure of Benedict Dingle Flint.

They pulled him up the shore and wrapped him in a jacket. They slapped him on the back. 'Good old Flinty!'

they laughed, and Flint did his best to grin – he tried very hard, but didn't quite make it.

He was in shock.

'I knew I had to swim for it,' he told them eventually, 'as soon as I heard the patrol boat. I swam under water for as long as I could, and just hoped they wouldn't see my head when I came up for air. It was ages until the bomb went off – I'd practically made it to the rocks – and then this huge great wave came rushing towards me and swept me in!'

'Cool under fire,' muttered Aka. The rest of them grunted assent.

'Chip off the old block!' agreed the Master Blaster, and when he heard those magic words Flint actually did manage a grin.

Aka drove the boy home on a tractor. One of the perks of being a bandit was that you could help yourself to anything and call it 'requisitioning', so he requisitioned a big blue Fordson with red wheels from an irritated farmer and took the boy back to Honeysuckle Farm.

'Well done,' he said when he dropped him by the milk churns. 'Your dad would have been proud of you.'

That's how Flint was back in time for supper – which was just as well, because the shock had worn off and he was hungry. He sniffed and snuffed the scent of cooking. *Roast chicken . . . and what's that sweet scent – that expensive scent – that scent that reminds me of Mum?*

'I was classically trained, you know,' Tumbleweed informed Jock the Border Collie, who wagged his tail and rested his head on her knee. She was having much the same effect on Flint, only he did not have a tail to wag and was far too polite to rest his chin on her knee.

'I was the little one in *A Midsummer Night's Dream,*' she told them proudly. They were sitting round the kitchen table – the two boys, the two Sweeties, and their unexpected guest who had turned up in her usual unexpected way, looking for supper and a natter with two old pals.

'At Stratford-upon-Avon?' asked Flossie.

'Not quite, we were on tour – starting in Belfast – then across to Glasgow – then down to the Bristol Hippodrome – then up again to Derby – and over to the Theatre Royal, Huddersfield. Finally we ended up in Guildford.'

'Guildford?' cried Alfie. 'Were you in the audience, Flinty?'

'No,' Flint managed to reply. Sitting next to Tumbleweed had a numbing effect on him. 'No,' he repeated, a little louder. 'We went to see *Aladdin,*' he explained shyly, 'but not *A Midsummer Night's Dream.*'

'I was in *Aladdin* too!' laughed Tumbleweed.

'Which one were you?' asked Flint.

'The one who sang, "When You Wish Upon A Star".' Her bright eyes gleamed; her dark hair shone; she smiled her special magical smile – the one that seemed to say she was a friend to all the world, but especially to YOU!

'Did you boys know that I trained her?' said Cicely. 'When she was first recruited – this was just before the invasion. She started off as a Secret Sweetie. Then she worked her way up.'

'How did you do that, my dear?' asked Flossie. 'Just how *did* you work your way up?'

'Don't ask!'

'So, boys,' said Cicely. 'The patrol boat's been sunk and the coast is clear. Well done!'

'Flinty saw to that,' said Alfie.

'It was me who took him on his first mission,' said Tumbleweed. 'He looked very sweet in his tea cosy.'

Flint tried very hard not to blush – and he'd have quite possibly succeeded if Alfie had not blurted out, 'You're making him blush!'

They all turned their heads to examine the evidence.

'We could save on candles,' said Alfie helpfully. 'Just sit him on the mantelpiece and embarrass him!'

Tumbleweed insisted on being shown Three Corner Field and Flat Rock. She wanted to pay her respects to the Secret Sweetie who had been chased to her death. 'I knew her,' she told the boys as they took her through the field full of thistles. 'Her name was Helen. I helped train her.'

'Did you train lots of Secret Sweeties?' asked Flint.

'Dozens!'

'Tumbleweed . . .' said Flint hopefully. She ruffled his hair by way of reply. 'You know my dad was executed?' he said very softly. 'Well, as soon as they shot him the Gestapo came round to our house and arrested my mum – Roberta Flint.'

'Oh!' she cried. 'Bobby Flint!'

'Yes! Bobby Flint! They – they dragged her out of the

house. They pushed me back in. She was screaming.'

Tumbleweed exchanged a quick glance with Alfie. Neither of them said anything.

'I . . . I thought they'd taken her to one of their concentration camps,' the boy continued in a low voice. 'But our Sweeties told me she was rescued. Bandits in the north – they derailed the train she was on – and Cicely interviewed her to see if she was criminal or political, and she was political. But they don't really know what happened to her after that. Do you?'

'Yes,' said Tumbleweed. 'She was recruited.'

'Recruited into what?'

'Recruited like I was recruited – and you and Alfie, and your two lovely, ancient Sweeties. There's no reason you shouldn't know this, Benedict. She's alive and kicking. She's not in a position to come looking for you, but if and when I see her again I'll tell her you're alive and kicking too. I can't tell you any more than that. So the Flints went to the panto, did they? Did you enjoy it?'

Flint was agog to learn more about his mum, but he knew Tumbleweed had deliberately changed the subject because she couldn't tell him anything other than that she was alive. This was frustrating and comforting both at once. He sighed and answered her question. 'Yes,' he said. 'It was wonderful.'

'What about you, Alfie? Do you know what's happened to *your* mum and dad?'

'Dad's in a mass grave,' explained Alfie, 'next to the Dartford bypass – at least his body is. His soul is with the angels – that's for sure. He wouldn't be in hell – not Dad.'

'What about your mum?'

Alfie didn't want to talk about it.

Tumbleweed stood on Flat Rock and gazed at the waves as they surged towards the shore. 'Here?' she asked. 'You think she jumped in here?'

They nodded.

'HELEN!' she suddenly shouted. 'CAN YOU HEAR ME?' She was yelling at the sea; maybe she thought her friend's ghost was down there with the fishes that had fed on her. 'IT'S THE GOING DOWN OF THE SUN!' she cried, which was true – the sun was setting in the west. 'IT'S THE GOING DOWN OF THE SUN AND WE'RE REMEMBERING YOU!'

'And Old Kent,' said Flint. 'Remember him too.' He suddenly thought about the sailors on the patrol boat. 'And everyone,' he said softly, 'who's sleeping with the fishes.'

There was no reply, and when Flint looked up Tumbleweed had gone. She was running up the steep path – glancing at her watch – running towards her next big adventure. Flint turned to follow, but Alfie caught his arm. He too was looking at his watch.

'Stay here,' he said. 'I told you about the mission before we saw the patrol boat – the one where two boys are wanted to escort a team of ruffians upcountry? Well, this is where they're landing. And our orders are to meet them!'

'What sort of ruffians?'

'You'll see!'

The boys waited as the twilight darkened into night. Alfie refused to answer Flint's questions, and sat on the pebbles looking smug until he glanced once more at his watch and said, 'Time!' He stepped back into the shadow of the cliff and brought a torch out of his pocket. 'Visitors,' he explained, 'from under the ocean.' He pressed a button and the torch flashed. 'Stand out of the way, and look out to sea!'

Flint turned to see an answering flash. 'All going to plan,' smiled Alfie. 'Here they come!' Suddenly Flint could make out the shape of a rubber dinghy careening its way between the rocks. The sound of its outboard could be heard above the splash and pull of the waves on the pebbles.

The dinghy surged into the beach. A sailor leapt out to hold its blunt bow as six armed men got out after him and scrambled up the pebbles. Within seconds they had surrounded the two boys. Flint was stunned – too shocked and excited to fully understand what was happening, but dimly aware that the dinghy had been turned and was speeding back out to sea.

One of the armed strangers grabbed Alfie by his shoulder and brought his crooked nose close to the boy's ear. 'It was Christmas Day in the cookhouse – the happiest day of the year!' he hissed. Alfie just had to wink at Flint before whispering the correct response: 'It was Christmas day in the cookhouse, the happiest day of the year; men's hearts were full of gladness, and their bellies full of beer, when up spoke Private Shorthouse, his face as bold as brass, saying, "We don't want your Christmas pudding – you can stick it up your . . ."'

'. . . jumper,' finished the stranger with an eerie chuckle.

13

Edward VIII, the King-Emperor, was sulking. Why couldn't they leave him alone? He scowled at them all – the generals, the Gestapo goons, the politicians, and the diplomats – as they milled about drinking his champagne. Why were they always badgering and advising and poking their noses in? Why had they followed him out to Windsor Castle? He should be left alone to mourn his darling queen in solitude – not plagued and harassed. And who was this ghastly little Hun with the ears? What was he blathering about in his awful accent?

'We must take urgent steps,' Dr Six was saying. 'Our information is that SOE has sent a unit of the Special

Boat Section to England – a unit that specialises in capture and abduction. We do not know who their target is, but the betting is that it's you.'

'Me?'

'We must review your security, sir. I have no doubt that you are surrounded by spies and informants.'

'But my people love me,' cried the king, glancing at himself in the Venetian mirror. 'They always have. They admire me for the way I'm trying to smooth things over with Germany.' He pulled a Sobranie Cocktail out of his golden cigarette case (a gift from the Crown Prince of Romania), slotted it into his cigarette holder, and waited for the bat-eared one to prance nimbly forward to light it for him, but the funny little fellow just continued with his bleating.

'Yes, sir, but the terrorists are not interested in the people, and neither is your niece.'

'The Pretender?'

'They've had their pretend coronation,' the frightful fellow reminded him. 'Now they'll want to see the back of you before you can have the real one.'

'Elizabeth was such a sweet girl,' sighed the king, lighting the cigarette all by himself – a skill he had been taught as a boy by Queen Victoria, and never quite forgotten. 'Did you see her in the newsreels in that open coach? All those Mounties trotting along behind – a crown on her head – lovely smile. Now she's a traitor to her RIGHTFUL KING, but when she was a little girl she was such a darling!'

114

'I'm sure she still is,' agreed the frightful one. 'But she is under the thumb of Lord Blade and the rest of the traitors.'

'What if we were to assassinate her first?' suggested the king hopefully. It was quite wrong to say he was only concerned with pleasure and fashion. He had a flair for politics and strategic thought.

'That's what they want, sir. It's why they don't bother to guard her properly. They know assassinating a teenage girl would put us in a bad light. Lord Blade and his friends would milk it for propaganda. They'd say we'd shot her while she was praying in church, then they'd declare her little sister queen.'

'Princess Margaret?'

'She'd be perfect for them – young and pretty – a royal Shirley Temple – the Americans would lap it up.'

'We could get rid of her too.'

'We don't know where she is. They've probably got her hidden in a cave in New Zealand.'

It really wasn't fair. He was recognised as the King-Emperor by Germany, Italy, Spain, Japan, and all those little nations with funny names that recognised the genius of Adolf Hitler. Everything would be fine if only his own people would do the same. Instead they treated him as if *he* was the traitor. It was so silly – all he was trying to do was use his boyish charm to bring about peace and reconciliation.

He gave a nod of dismissal, but the ghastly Hun was too common and vulgar to take the hint. In the end Sir

Oswald, the Prime Minister of the New National Government, was forced to intervene. 'Thank you, Dr Six,' he said firmly. 'We have already reviewed security, and, thanks to your own orders, the castle is surrounded by a ring of steel. But His Majesty needs his rest.' At last Dr Six understood that he was no longer wanted, bowed, and backed out of the door.

'I've not been sleeping properly since the accident,' the king confided to Sir Oswald. 'Lord Dawson has been very good.' Lord Dawson was the King's physician. 'He's prescribed a sedative; I have to have an injection three times a day, and he's sent a very pretty nurse to do the jabbing.'

In her clean and tidy preparation room close to the king's quarters deep in the heart of Windsor Castle the pretty nurse was listening to the wireless:

Fierce fighting continues in Moscow, announced the newsreader solemnly, *where the Second Panzer Army is reported to have occupied the Kremlin.* The little nurse began to arrange her equipment – the sedative, the syringe and the needle. *At home, security forces have launched an anti-terrorist drive in the south-west,* the newsreader continued blandly. *Dr Franz Six, Chief of Security Police, told a press conference today that so far 643 insurgents had been either killed or captured.*

'Lies, lies, lies!' muttered the nurse with a frown. 'What complete and utter codswallop!'

Buckingham Palace today announced the revised date for

the Coronation, which will now take place in Westminster Abbey on August the third. A spokesman confirmed that among world leaders expected to attend are Adolf Hitler, the German Chancellor, and President Amos Q Pearmouth of the United States.

'Don't bet on it!'

It is hoped, now that Great Britain is a partner in the Pan-European Alliance and the war in the west has ended, that representatives from Canada, Australia and New Zealand will attend the king's coronation and the ceremony will mark a final end to hostilities. It is also understood that the king has issued personal invitations to his nieces Princess Elizabeth and Princess Margaret.

The nurse pulled a face.

Preparations are under way for the traditional ceremony of Swan Upping on the Thames at Windsor . . .

Tumbleweed jumped – that was the signal!

The snatch squad had arrived!

14

It had taken them a week to get from Honeysuckle Farm to Windsor. All the way from Bradford on Avon they'd travelled by narrowboat. This is why, when SOE had planned Operation King's Ransom back in St John's, they'd contacted Dart Patrol and requested two boys – so that a barge full of commandos could glide calmly through occupied England crewed by two barge boys. Now their narrowboat was moored unobtrusively under the battlements of Windsor Castle, and Flint was seeing to the horse.

Flint waited until Beauty had finished drinking before tying on the nosebag. Then he patted her neck. He did that for his own benefit; it was good being close to the huge, contented animal. It had a calming effect, and the munching sound was deeply reassuring.

Swans were still gliding elegantly down river and, even though the light was fading, ducklings were still doing important duckling stuff. The wind rustled the willows, and beyond them Flint could make out the turrets of the great castle, dark against the red sky. He darted down the towpath and stepped lightly aboard the *Lady Sylvia*. She rocked gently as he made his way down the steps into the little cabin, where he lit one of the oil lamps and put the kettle on. Beyond the cabin a canvas awning covered the narrowboat's cargo of freshly sawn oak timbers, under which the six commandos waited in expectant silence.

Flint knew that they'd come for the king, and he knew that the chances of success were SLIM, while the chances of ending up in a shallow grave were MASSIVE. He had a far-away feeling that this might be his last night on earth, and that he'd die without ever finding his mother.

When the kettle boiled he made himself a mug of tea and clambered back on deck. Alfie's furtive figure was slinking down the towpath towards him, lugging two bulging shopping bags. Every so often Alfie stopped and stood very still to listen and peer about. Every so often he'd glance at his fancy watch before pushing it back up his sleeve out of sight. The closer the furtive figure came to the *Lady Sylvia*, the more theatrical these gestures became. Flint knew that the performance was for his benefit; the swans and the ducks certainly weren't interested.

Alfie tiptoed towards the barge with exaggerated, clown-like caution. 'The geese fly south!' he hissed.

'Very funny!' Of course, it wasn't a real code; it was just Alfie hamming it up. He'd been buzzing with excitement ever since the snatch squad had jumped ashore at Honeysuckle Cove. Alfie had gone a long way up in his own estimation: he'd jumped from farm slave to bandit to brigand, and all in a matter of weeks. Ordinary, boring bandits did ordinary bandit stuff like blowing up trucks. Brigands captured kings!

Alfie bounced jauntily aboard, rummaged into one of the bags and handed Flint a helping of fish and chips rolled up in newspaper. Then he looked cautiously up and down the river before clambering round the cabin to the cargo hold, where he hissed again: 'The geese fly south in winter!' The hidden snatch squad commandos thought this was funny; they laughed under their awning, a sinister sound like briskly boiling blood.

A hand, attached to a muscular arm, reached out from under the canvas and tugged in a bag of bottles. A low voice growled, 'Where's the opener?'

'You're supposed to be tough,' was Alfie's answer. 'Use your teeth!' They thought that was funny too.

It was Flint who found them the bottle opener. It was grabbed from him with a low rumble of thanks. The bag full of fish and chips had already disappeared into the hold, and soon a contented silence, punctuated only by rustling newspaper, descended on the *Lady Sylvia*.

Two German soldiers appeared, walking down the towpath. They paused by the munching horse and turned to inspect the narrowboat. Flint whistled 'It's a Long Way to Tipperary', which was the warning tune. The six commandos hidden under the timber heard him and came silently on guard. Alfie himself drew his beloved Fairbairn fighting knife and secreted it out of sight under the gangway. He took a sip from his mug and put it down on deck just above the knife, then gave the soldiers a friendly grin.

One of them was tall, broad-shouldered and blond, but with a dim expression on his bland face. The other one looked like a tortoise on stilts.

Alfie summed them up as *easy*, but he did not want trouble. He did not want to make a disturbance – and neither did Flint, who was watching nervously from the cabin. There were Nazi soldiers all round the castle. Flint had seen dozens of them, but none had paid the innocent-looking barge any attention. The two guards looked relaxed. Alfie greeted them with a friendly *'Heil Hitler!'* and offered them some chips.

The pair responded gratefully; they'd been pulled out of bandit territory to join the ring of steel round Windsor and were enjoying the change of scenery.

Flint watched as the soldiers ate their chips. Alfie seemed to be fearless – effortlessly fearless. There he sat, cool and confident, a brigand in a boat full of brigands, and what did he do when the enemy turned up? He put his knife in a handy position in case of unpleasantness, and offered them some chips!

You had to be impressed.

Now the soldiers were moving away, waving their thanks, and Alfie was checking his watch.

'SOON!' he mouthed to Flint. 'WE GO INTO ACTION SOON!'

15

r Six's socks went into the stainless-steel laundry bin, followed by his fly-fronted novelty underpants – the ones with Winston Churchill's head on the seat. He was back in London, in his rooms in the Albany, and it was past midnight. Stark naked apart from his thick pebble glasses, he poured himself a glass of *Wurzelpeter*, blinked, and lowered himself into the bath. The pebble glasses steamed over, but Dr Six did not remove them; he lay back in the hot water and brooded. He guessed that at least half of his Death Squad chiefs distrusted him – and all because he'd had a couple of slackers shot and three more posted to the Russian front.

Dr Franz Alfred Six closed his eyes and began to count his blessings. He raised the glass to his thin lips, took a swig . . . and frowned, because he could not think of any. There had been a time, not long ago, when he had been a Nazi star. His death squads had brought immediate and radical change to Occupied English Territory. Surviving males between the ages of seventeen and forty-five had been given the opportunity to work in the Fatherland, criminals and other undesirables had been quietly eliminated, and a firm foundation for a new and improved England had been established.

To crown his early achievements, it had been Dr Six who had saved Hitler's life in Trafalgar Square; he'd seen the barrel of the assassin's gun and shoved him to the ground. And it had been Franz Alfred Six himself who had commanded the firing squad that had executed the would-be assassin – the M9 boffin Flint. The Führer had watched the shooting and congratulated him. That December day in 1940 had been the highpoint of Dr Six's career; since then there had been nothing but problems, and all the time his enemies among the Gestapo chiefs plotted against him. He certainly distrusted Count Kasimir von dem Wappenbuch.

A snatch squad, he brooded. *First Queen Wallis meets with an accident, and then they send out a snatch squad. Why would they want to capture the royal fool? Why not simply put a bullet through his vain brain, or poison the dapper little idiot? If it was me*, thought Six, *I'd have bumped off the pair of them in a single fake accident.*

One thing he knew for sure: if SOE got hold of the king it would be a huge blow to the German war effort. Lord Blade had been desperately trying to trick the Americans into the war, but so far the puppet king and his American queen had given them the perfect excuse not to intervene. But now Queen Wallis was dead and, somewhere in England, a snatch squad was closing in. This was why a thousand SS Storm Troopers were within the walls of Windsor Castle; why a further three thousand infantry patrolled the town and the surrounding countryside; why you would need a small army, a miniature air force, and a lot of luck to capture the king.

It was dark. Flint and Alfie had run up and down the towpath and reported that the coast was clear. Now the six commandos were emerging from their hiding place, stretching and checking their weapons. One belched; another yawned; the grinning thug with the crooked nose spat; another scratched himself in an unmentionable place; their officer swore under his breath; the sergeant farted.

Alfie watched, his face alight with excitement. He wanted to accompany them, of course, but the commandos indicated by subtle two-fingered gestures that they could manage without him.

Flint watched quietly. Whenever he thought he was about to die he went very quiet. He sat in the cabin and waited.

Alfie was checking his watch.

Perhaps Dad had a special watch, thought Flint. *In Trafalgar Square.* He tried to imagine it. *What would he have said? What would his last words have been? He'd have said something funny. He'd have scorned a blindfold and said, 'What frabjous fun!' Something like that.*

Flint had a lot to live up to.

The commandos jumped ashore; the boat rocked. Boots crunched on the towpath as the snatch squad disappeared into the trees that crested the rising ground between the river and the castle.

Flint glanced at Alfie. Alfie nodded, and Flint stepped lightly on to the bank.

The King-Emperor smiled impishly. He sat on the end of his four-poster bed in a silk dressing gown and radiated charm.

'If you changed out of that uniform and dressed up in a crinoline you'd look just like Scarlett O'Hara in *Gone With the Wind*,' he told the nurse. 'But you'd need red ribbons instead of that absurd hat.'

'There's nothing absurd about my cap,' replied the nurse sternly.

'It makes you look like a nun. With a face like yours you should have flowers in your hair.'

'I'm a nurse, not a southern belle.' She gave him her Florence Nightingale look and checked the syringe. 'Now,' she allowed him a quick smile, 'this won't hurt!' She administered the injection and waited alertly for it to take effect.

Then she called for an ambulance.

'Heart attack!' The news spread round the castle.

'Heart attack,' the prime minister informed Dr Six. He lowered his voice and hissed down the phone. 'Thank God his nurse was there when it happened. What? Yes – she's in the ambulance with him. They should be at St Thomas' hospital within the hour. Let's hope he doesn't die on the way – we need the little creep!'

'Good work, Tumbleweed!' laughed the driver, as the ambulance rattled down the road away from Windsor. Four motorcycle outriders raced ahead of it, and a Gestapo Mercedes brought up the rear – until the ambulance suddenly skidded sharply off the main road and shot unexpectedly down the B3026 towards Eton Wick.

The motorcycles sped on without it, and the Mercedes slammed on its brakes.

After about fifty yards the outriders realised the ambulance was no longer behind them. They yelled, gesticulated, spun round, and headed back. The Mercedes stood silent at the junction, its windscreen shattered. The driver was slumped over the wheel, a neat hole in his skull. The passengers were sprawled over the seats. They looked shocked, limp and dead.

The outriders drew their pistols. They conferred. They put the pistols back in their holsters and set off after the ambulance in hot pursuit. Down the road they sped, four abreast, towards the river. Rounding a corner they caught sight of the fleeing ambulance. They accelerated –

fifty – sixty – seventy – eighty . . .

They'd just touched eighty miles an hour when they hit the wire.

The King-Emperor opened his eyes. The sweet nurse was looking down at him, but she was not smiling – the strict Florence Nightingale look was back on her pretty face. A twist of fear disturbed him; something must have happened, something bad. He was in some sort of vehicle. They were lurching, rattling and swaying through the night.

'You're awake!' she said.

'What's happening?'

'We've rescued you.'

'Rescued me from what?' He was still woozy from the knock-out jab, but fear clears the head. He was alert enough now to guess how she'd reply. But she didn't reply. Instead a cheerful voice cut in – the driver's voice.

'From the Huns, old chap.'

The King-Emperor did not respond immediately. There was something chilling about that cheery voice calling him *old chap*. You don't call kings *old chap* – unless, of course, you're a rebel. He attempted to marshal his thoughts. 'But I'm negotiating with them.'

'Not any more!' replied the driver.

'You're going to execute me, aren't you?'

'If we just wanted you dead I'd have given you a lethal injection,' replied the nurse briskly. She turned away from him and peered ahead. 'There they are!' she cried.

The ambulance skidded to a standstill. Its back doors were flung open. There stood the snatch squad – and would you believe it?

None of them bowed!

The King-Emperor was pulled roughly onto the road. He recognised the woods it ran through; they were near the river. He gasped as the tip of a bayonet was pushed gently but firmly through his silk dressing gown until the delicate skin of the royal rump was slightly punctured. A trickle of royal blood ran down the king's left leg and seeped into the imperial pyjamas. He was surrounded by soldiers – ugly thugs with bust noses, scars and tin hats. Out of the corner of his eye the king could see the ambulance driver and the nurse in close consultation with two middle-aged civilians. He didn't ask himself who they might be or what they might be doing.

The two men clambered into the ambulance.

'Local Resistance,' explained the nurse as she watched them turn the vehicle and set off back towards the main road. 'Don't worry,' she smiled. 'Everything's going to plan!'

Dr Six looked at the decapitated bodies of the motor-cyclists and cursed. He glanced down the road towards the bridge in the early morning light. 'Has the ambulance been found?' he asked a soldier.

'Not yet, sir.'

'They'll have abandoned it by now,' he said thoughtfully. 'They'll have transferred to another vehicle.'

'We've ringed the town with roadblocks as you instructed – and there's more at five-mile intervals for twenty miles.'

'What's that?' Six pointed in the direction of the river, where a boy was leading a horse pulling a barge. The Gestapo chief peered intently through his glasses. 'Look,' he yelled excitedly. 'Look at that barge! I know how their minds work. They enjoy making us look like fools. We've blocked and double-blocked every road leading out of this town; we've got thousands of troops patrolling through the countryside – so how do they get the king away?'

'Down the river?'

'Down the river!'

Flint was leading the horse – not that she needed leading – when he heard an urgent yell.

'Stop!' ordered an angry, bat-eared Gestapo goon who was running towards them. He came abreast of the *Lady Sylvia*. 'Stop!' he ordered again. 'I am Dr Six, Gestapo Chief for English Occupied Territory!'

'What is it, sir?' Alfie shouted helpfully from the tiller. 'Do you want to buy some timber, sir? I'm not allowed to sell none, sir – we got to take it to Bristol.'

'Come in to the land!' yelled Dr Six. 'Stop your ship!'

'Jimmy!' called Alfie.

Flint turned to face them. He blinked. He assumed the innocent, ever-so-slightly gormless expression of the little one in Laurel and Hardy. Half a dozen German soldiers were now waiting to jump aboard the boat as well as the Gestapo Chief for Occupied English Territory.

He glared at Flint.

'*Halt!*' he ordered. 'Stop your horse!'

Alfie skipped confidently ashore and helped bring the *Lady Sylvia* to the bank. 'He's mute, sir,' he confided to Dr Six, pointing proudly at Flint as if he was showing off a fairground freak. Behind him the soldiers began to peel back the canvas awning. 'He don't talk,' grinned the cheerful boy, 'but he can whistle.'

Flint stood pale and silent by the horse's head, watching as Dr Six stepped aboard the barge and strutted forward to inspect the hold. He peered keenly through his glasses as the soldiers shifted the timber.

It struck the good doctor as exactly the sort of place someone would hide a kidnapped king.

16

F lint watched anxiously as the soldiers searched the hold. *What if they find all the empty beer bottles?* he asked himself. *What will they say about the old fish-and-chip wrappings and the stubbed-out cigarettes? They'll know it's not just our mess . . . They'll guess the snatch squad was there . . .*

Alfie must have been thinking the same thing, because he sauntered up behind Dr Six and tapped him on the shoulder. 'Would you like to hear the mute whistle, sir? Jimmy!' he yelled at Flint. 'Whistle for the gentleman!'

The startled boy standing next to the horse gaped, but did not whistle. 'He's shy, sir,' explained Alfie. A long, soothing noise came from Flint's direction. 'That weren't him, sir,' Alfie added, 'that were the horse, farting.'

Dr Six wheeled round. He stood nose to nose with young Alfred Scott and he told him exactly what he thought of farting horses and whistling mutes – which was not much!

Flint listened as Alfie answered back. *Why doesn't he just keep his mouth shut?* he asked himself anxiously. *I suppose he's doing it as a distraction.*

'It's the diet, sir, it's all the hay,' Alfie was telling Dr Six. 'It builds up wind, sir. I'm talking about the horse, sir, not the mute.'

No missing king was discovered in the *Lady Sylvia's* cargo hold. And Alfie had succeeded in distracting Dr Six, who never saw the snatch squad's rubbish. Of course, the searching soldiers saw it, but paid no attention; what would empty beer bottles have to do with kings?

Dr Six bristled with frustration. He jumped back onto the towpath and glared at the two idiot boys until a tiny little soldier, looking like a tortoise on stilts, came running down the towpath from the direction of the bridge. The ambulance had been found – pushed into a gravel pit.

'Where?' asked Franz Alfred Six. 'Where is this gravel pit?'

'Staines.'

'Reinforce the ring of steel between Staines and London. Start house-to-house searches in every town and village in that area. Shift troops into the western suburbs!'

'What about the river?'

'Guard every lock and search every barge from Staines to the Pool of London!'

'That was a narrow shave!' hissed Alfie as soon as they were gone. '*And* they've delayed us.' He glanced at his watch.

The two boys had to meet up with Tumbleweed, the snatch squad and their prisoner in less than twenty minutes. It was part of the plan. They'd been told they'd be given something that was vital to the war effort. They were to smuggle it out of danger. Those were their orders, and now they were going to be late.

Flint tugged urgently at Beauty's bridle and soon the *Lady Sylvia* was surging up river. He knew they had to keep going for just over a mile, but Alfie had the map. He could see him at the tiller, alternatively squinting at it and checking their surroundings. 'OK!' Alfie called eventually.

Flint slowed the barge to a stop and busied himself making it fast to the bank with mooring pins. Soon the two boys were hurrying through the fields; their orders were to meet the others in the woods that ran along the ridge of hills beyond. They had the map reference, and Alfie still had the map in his maimed hand. Again he consulted his watch and glanced at the map.

'Faster,' he hissed. 'We're supposed to be there by now.'

A track went through the woods and met the road at a farm gate. That was the rendezvous – it was where the boys should have been.

'Something's happened to them!' muttered Tumble-weed. 'And where are the local bandits?'

She glanced at the king in his silk dressing gown; he was sitting on a tree stump, surrounded by the bayonets of the grinning snatch squad. The two boys were needed now. If they'd been arrested or killed there would have to be a Plan B. And where were the two local bandits? All they'd had to do was get rid of the ambulance and turn up at the rendezvous with the hearse. So why were they so late?

'Here they come,' replied G106 as a black Rover glided through the open gate and parked on the track, followed by a gleaming hearse. One of the local resistance men alighted from the Rover, while the other one jumped down from the hearse. They were dressed in sombre dark suits; they wore black ties.

Each of them carried a wreath.

The snatch squad greeted Flint and Alfie with friendly grins when they arrived at the rendezvous nearly ten minutes late. The boys were panting and puffing, and Flint had a stitch. He gaped in surprise at the forlorn figure of King Edward VIII squatting on his tree stump. The boys had worked out that he was the one the snatchers had been sent to snatch; even so, it seemed so very shocking to see him in his dressing gown.

And there was Tumbleweed – the beautiful, bright-eyed Tumbleweed. Of course, they were pleased to see her, especially when she gave them a welcoming wave and blew them a kiss.

'See that bloke she's talking to,' whispered Alfie, 'the bloke with the Brylcreem and the grin – that's her boss.'

'Boss? I thought the queen was her boss.'

'That's the famous G106. He comes down to see Aka now and then, and he's always in on anything big – and you can't get bigger than this!' He cocked his head in the direction of the royal tree stump.

'What's he doing?' whispered Flint. 'What's all that equipment?'

Alfie shook his head. 'I don't know,' he said, 'but we'll soon find out.'

The dapper G106 was squinting down a spring-wound clockwork cine camera, while Tumbleweed was busy connecting the microphone to the tape recorder and fiddling about with what looked like a car battery. The king watched them warily, as if he was trying to work out what they were up to. It seemed strange to Flint to be so close to someone so famous – so instantly recognisable – although the king was not looking his usual relaxed and charming self. 'Ready?' asked G106.

The king glanced down the barrels of six Thompson submachine guns, and then into the mocking eyes of the men that held them.

'Here is your script,' said Tumbleweed, handing him a sheet of paper. 'Just look into the camera and read it out.'

'Action!' cried G106, clicking switches, checking dials, and squinting down the viewfinder.

Flint saw the king take a deep breath and smile sadly into the camera.

'I was living in Portugal at the time of my brother's death,' he read gravely. 'There I was approached by the British government – by what I knew to be a puppet government under the thumb of the occupying power. They begged me to accept the crown. They said – and I agreed with them at the time – that I was uniquely placed to bring about peace and reconciliation with Germany. It was with such hopes and aspirations that I accepted.'

As the King-Emperor read on, Flint noticed Tumbleweed move towards the parked Rover. She opened the boot, took out a bag and disappeared behind the car. Two minutes later she reappeared. Gone was the nurse's uniform: now she was dressed entirely in black.

It was as if she was about to attend a funeral.

The six thugs encouraged the anxious king by fingering their weapons threateningly. He continued.

'I sincerely believed that it was possible to work with Germany,' he said sadly. 'But I was wrong. For several months I pleaded with Hitler to send all British captives home. He refused.

'Finally I gave the Germans an ultimatum. I told them that unless my demands were met I would abdicate. They laughed in my face. I knew that they had executed my brother. I had reason to suspect that they were responsible for the death of my wife. I was left with no alternative but to escape.

'So here I am, somewhere in England – and here I will

stay until either they hunt me down or we have victory. Germany is locked in a death struggle with the Russians. She bleeds. She weakens hour by hour and day by day. Meanwhile, the British Resistance grows stronger. It is to their cause that I shall dedicate the remainder of my days. God save the Queen!'

'Cut!' cried G106, which struck Flint as odd. Since he was the cameraman, he was talking to himself.

Flint watched as the eccentric agent brandished a spool of film in the air. That must be what he and Alfie had to smuggle to bandit country, but he'd not worked out why it was so important.

G106 must have seen his bewildered expression. 'Political warfare,' he explained. 'The traitor king sees the error of his ways – escapes – joins the Resistance! People will lap it up from Adelaide to Little Rock.'

'Will they?' sighed the king. He glanced at the hearse, his eyes resting on the wreaths.

'Oh yes,' Tumbleweed assured him. 'Our little film will show in every news theatre in the free world. It will be a triumph of propaganda.'

She fished about in her bag and pulled out her syringe.

Flint saw the look of horror on the king's pale face and hissed at Alfie. 'What's she going to do with that?'

Alfie pointed at the shining, black hearse with an oak coffin in the back. 'That must be how they're going to get him away,' he whispered, 'in that coffin!'

'You mean she's going to kill him?'

'They won't do that,' Alfie replied, 'unless they have

to. There's a ring of steel all round here, isn't there? Hundreds of soldiers are out searching for him – road-blocks on all the roads – so that's how they're going to slip through.'

'Slip through?'

'Slip through the ring of steel, Flinty, disguised as a funeral cortege.'

'You mean they think soldiers at a roadblock would just wave them through?' asked Flint doubtfully.

'They will when the weeping widow pleads with them.'

'And if they don't?'

'There'll be unpleasantness. That must be why we're all going our separate ways. The hearse is going in one direction, carrying the king, with Tumbleweed in the back of the Rover weeping into her hanky. The snatchers are going in another, and our job is obviously to smuggle the film out along the canal, so if the others get caught at least the king's little speech will find its way to Newfoundland. It won't be easy,' he warned. 'There'll be checkpoints and lots of inquisitive soldiers. That's why the commandos won't be aboard. They'll be on their own until we pick them up again halfway down the canal. Things will be quieter down there.'

Tumbleweed's injection worked like a charm. OK, the thugs in the tin hats had to hold the king down, and he kicked up a bit of a fuss, but as soon as she jabbed the needle into the left cheek of his bum he stopped screaming.

In fact, he went very quiet.

Flint watched as the limp body was dumped into the coffin and wondered with a shudder whether it was alive or dead.

'An excellent performance,' laughed G106, tapping the metal case containing his spool of undeveloped film and bowing ironically towards the coffin. He sauntered across the clearing towards the boys. 'Here it is,' he said, handing the spool to Flint. 'Your job is to smuggle it out along the canal. Then you hand it over to the snatch squad when you meet them again. They'll take it back to Newfoundland.'

'Yes, sir,' replied Alfie smartly. 'Flint here has worked out exactly where to hide it – somewhere they'll never think of looking – not that they'll be looking for a spool anyway. They'll be looking for the king.'

'Flint?' asked the SOE man.

'This is Flint, sir. Don't be fooled by his gormless look – that's just his way, sir, his cunning way. This is the legendary Benedict Dingle Flint, sir, the bandit.'

The young outlaw blinked shyly.

'Flint, old chap,' said G106, in very much the same tone that Squadron Leader James Bigglesworth, DSO, DFC, MC might have used to greet his old pal Captain the Honourable Algernon Lacey, MC. 'Was your father Dingle Flint? Yes?' He shook Flint's hand and thumped his back. 'My dear chap! I was with your dad in M9 – back before the invasion – "Fearless Flint" we called him!'

Flint gulped proudly.

'Cunning as a fox force-fed on fish! What fun we had in

the old days! Well, well, well. Dingle Flint – a very enter-taining fellow – played the piano!'

'Yes, sir.'

'And it was not so very long ago that I ran into your dear mother!'

'Where?' yelped Flint. A wave of joy lifted his spirits.

'On the other side of the pond – but duty calls, lads. They're waiting for me. Toodle-oo!'

The boys watched the cortege drive away with the king in the coffin.

'They're taking him to a safe house,' guessed Alfie. 'They probably want to keep him alive to make more films.'

Flint nodded absently – he wasn't really listening. 'What pond?' he asked. 'What pond is my mum on the other side of?'

'The Atlantic Ocean. She'll be in Newfoundland,' Alfie announced confidently, 'with the queen!'

17

Flint had plenty of time to brood about Newfoundland. The *Lady Sylvia* only went as fast as a horse could walk, and they had miles to go before they reached Bradford on Avon. For mile after mile Flint was able to dream:

The lovely Lady Tumbleweed turned to the legendary outlaw. 'Oh Benedict!' she sighed. 'Surely you do not intend to cross the Atlantic Ocean on a horse-drawn barge!'

'Indeed I do,' the young brigand chuckled. 'But instead of a horse I shall use a mast and sails. Never forget, my lady, that long before I was an outlaw I was a fighter ace, and before that I was a midshipman. Besides I won't be sailing

across single-handed; I'm taking my batman.'

'Alfie? What possible use could he be, except for shining your shoes?'

'He may not have much between the ears, but the poor chap means well. And he's a dab hand at catching fish!'

'Trouble ahead!' hissed Alfie. Flint glanced apprehensively up the towpath. A posse of German soldiers was watching them from a nearby road bridge.

'Halt!' the sergeant yelled. One of them began to walk over the bridge towards the gate that led down to the river.

The boys brought the boat to the bank and waited. The gate opened, and two very familiar soldiers came loping down the slope towards them – one so small his helmet had not shown above the parapet.

Flint could not help but glance at the secret place where he'd hidden the spool. *Don't look in that direction!* he instructed himself as the two soldiers began searching the boat. He watched as Hans examined the timbers.

'Wood,' said Hans, whose English was improving. 'Wood heavy – boys move wood.' A wide grin spread itself over his big, bland face.

'Chips?' Wolfgang was asking. 'Do you have the chips?'

Flint shook his head and Alfie assumed the deeply friendly expression he always used when dealing with the enemy. Soon both boys were unloading the timber. Since the commandos were not due to join them until they'd left the Thames, they weren't worried.

Eventually the two soldiers were satisfied that no one

was in the hold, and returned to their bridge. The two young bandits reloaded the timber and resumed their voyage.

They were stopped and searched twice more that day, even though they were heading westward, but this did not worry them, because the spool of film was hidden at the bottom of Beauty's nosebag.

'Brilliant, Flinty,' said Alfie. 'No one would think of looking for it there.'

'No,' agreed Flint. He was sitting at the stern taking a turn at the tiller. 'In fact, they're not even looking for it, are they?'

'Suppose not.' Alfie sipped from his mug of tea and Flint returned to his dreams:

Firebrand Flint, at twelve years old the youngest trooper in the North West Mounted Police, kicked Turpin's flanks and spurred forward to meet the war party. With his right hand raised in greeting he rode fearlessly towards their fabled leader Grey Wolf, Paramount Chief of the Mohawks.

'Hail Great Chief!' cried the young red-coat.

'Lord Blade was right to entrust the film to us, Flinty,' said Alfie proudly. 'We look innocent and we're doing something normal – transporting a load of wood.'

'Do you think the others will make it?' asked Flint anxiously.

'Possibly,' replied Alfie with a shrug.

Their orders were to pick up the snatch squad at Cobbler's Lock, halfway down the Kennet and Avon

Canal and many miles from Windsor. Flint was still dreaming about his mother as they approached this rendezvous by moonlight. *I should have asked Tumbleweed to take her a message,* he thought sadly. *She's always going to and from St. John's, and she seems to know all about Mum even if she won't say much about her.*

'Nearly there!' warned Alfie. 'I wonder if they've made it.'

'There they are!' cried Flint. What was left of the snatch squad – four men – emerged from the cover of the trees, waving nonchalantly in the moonlight as the Lady Sylvia nosed into the bank. Then they flitted in single file on to her deck before making for their place in the hold.

'Firefight,' explained one as he passed Flint. 'We lost two good men.'

'There was no time to bury them,' muttered the commando behind him. 'And we've not slept for a week!'

For the next two days the snatchers slumbered and snored under the canvas awning while the boys guided the barge westward towards their rendezvous with the Resistance.

Three figures were waiting for them near Bradford on Avon – the man who had lent the barge, his wife, and the bandit in charge of Shepton Patrol – a sharp young man with a Sten gun across his back. This was where they were to hand back the *Lady Sylvia* and continue on foot to Dart Patrol territory, fifty miles to the west. That was where the four surviving commandos and the precious spool of film would embark across the pond.

Flint slowed the horse down and the barge glided smoothly into the bank; the woman stepped aboard and took over the tiller from Alfie. They exchanged nods. Then Alfie jumped cheerfully onto the towpath, followed by the four yawning commandos. Flint said goodbye to Beauty, but not before removing the spool from her nosebag, and the *Lady Sylvia* continued her voyage to Bristol as if nothing remarkable had ever happened.

The bandit known as Sharp led the depleted snatch squad, Alfie and Flint to his Operational Base. The Resistance had OBs where they kept their folding motorbikes, exploding rats, submachine guns and sabotage equipment. OBs were where bandits ate and slept; they couldn't live their secret lives among the people or they'd be shipped out as slaves. This is why they smelt so very distinctive.

They'd made the rendezvous by about noon, so there was still plenty of daylight left. Flint was worried. So was Sharp. Flint could tell he would have much preferred to have been lying deep in a ditch under a tree in the middle of a forest at midnight on a starless night. Wandering about in the sunshine with a bunch of thugs in Alberta boots made him twitch and wince.

Sharp moved like a shadow – he reminded Flint of Aka. He shuddered whenever he heard a twig snap, and a lot of twigs were snapping.

'Do we have far to go?' whispered Flint, who was scuttling alongside the bandit, trying to keep up with his long strides. He rattled a bit when he ran, on account of the

146

film canister, which he carried under his shirt.

The bandit looked down at the boy with surprise. He put a finger to his lips and frowned. Then he glared at the four commandos, who grinned back at him. 'What's the matter, Worzel? We making too much noise?'

'I thought you lot were Special Forces!' hissed the bandit.

'We are, mate – very special!'

'Well, why do you move over the ground like a herd of elephants, then?'

'Because we're amphibious – we're not used to land, but we swim very quietly.'

'What do you mean, amphibious?'

'Special Boat Section!' they told him proudly.

Sharp shuddered.

The worried bandit led them cautiously out of the trees. He stopped. He listened. He looked about. They were in the corner of a narrow, steeply sloping field; sheep bleated and scattered as the party followed him in the shade of the hedgerow. Here Sharp stopped at a feeding trough full of hay. He looked about once more before shoving the hay to one side, revealing what looked like a manhole cover. He pressed what appeared to be a nail head, then pushed; the cover slid easily to one side on well-greased runners.

'Right,' he whispered, looking at Flint. 'Down you go!'

18

Flint tapped at the spool just to make sure it was still there, then he scrambled down a set of metal rungs into an underground chamber. Light streamed in from portholes set into the thick reinforced walls. Looking through one, Flint realised that he was squinting along a narrow tunnel which burrowed through the side of the hill until it broke into the grass where the sheep were grazing. To anyone walking through that sloping field they'd have looked exactly like what they were supposed to look like: rabbit holes.

The underground base had a lived-in atmosphere. There were bunks complete with rumpled army blankets.

No pillows – no sheets – this was an OB, not the Ritz. The place smelt of the chemical toilet and paraffin from the cooking stove and the Tilley lamps. Stacks of stores and a churn of water stood in one corner; arms, ammunition and sabotage material were stacked in another. There was a kitchen table with a trench phone, surrounded by folding chairs. A map of the North Atlantic was stuck to a wall, showing British controlled territory from Newfoundland to the Shetlands, and a local map was spread out on the table together with a book called *The Countryman's Diary*.

Flint had seen *The Countryman's Diary* before; there'd been a copy in the Bolt Hole. It explained just how to make a small amount of explosives go a very long way. Drawings and diagrams showed how to fill cocoa tins with gelignite, then bury them in biscuit tins full of stones and nails. There were sections on the best way to blow up armoured cars, tanks, and aircraft on the ground. It recommended cunning techniques for booby traps and gave strict instruction about how to set fire to ammunition dumps up-wind.

'This is amazing,' whispered Flint. 'It must have been built just before the invasion.'

'Lots of them were,' replied Alfie. 'That's what Doc told me. They dug them all over the place.'

If the boys were impressed, the snatch squad most definitely was not. 'This is worse than that sub!' one of them said – the one with a bullet hole in his ear.

'We've just spent three days and nights squatting

under a pile of wood,' growled another, 'now Worzel here wants us to live down a rat hole!'

Sharp glared and muttered under his breath. This was Shepton Patrol's Operational Base. It was where they slept, ate and planned, when they weren't out causing havoc. They'd given up their sleeping quarters so that the snatch squad could rest. All the local bandits – apart from Sharp himself – were kipping out in haystacks so that the commandos could have some peace and security. The least they could do was say thanks.

Instead of stretching out on the bunks, the commandos sat round the table in the folding chairs and showed Alfie how to play poker. Sharp, who'd been up all night silencing informants and derailing the odd train, gave them one last glare before climbing into a bunk, wrapping himself in blankets and falling instantly to sleep.

Flint followed the young bandit's example, and soon he was dreaming once more:

Two men looked down into Trafalgar Square from the dome on top of the National Gallery. One of them wore glasses.

This was one of Flint's most deep and private dreams – the one about his father's death. He hadn't been there when it had happened, of course, but he'd learnt some of the facts, and what he didn't know he imagined. For example, Flint knew there'd been a sniper called McNab, but had no idea what he'd looked like. This was why in his dream McNab kept changing. First he appeared with a shock of red hair, a wild beard, and eyebrows like the wings of a soaring vulture. Next he had a shaved head and tattooed arms. But Flint had no problems visualising McNab's companion – the man in the glasses – the one who was saying, 'Jolly good!'

'Jolly good!' whispered F3. 'They're getting out of the car – and there's Uncle Adolf!'

The sniper squinted down the barrel of his Lee-Enfield .303; Hitler's head appeared smack in the sights, but before he could fire a shot another head was in the way. 'Get out of it!' growled McNab. For several seconds the sniper waited for a clear shot. He'd have done better to pull the trigger – the bullet might have gone right through the intruding head and into the heart of Adolf Hitler. But that's not what happened.

Footsteps – boots on marble steps!

McNab wheeled round as they burst into the chamber. He got in one shot before he fell in a hail of lead. They pounced on F3, knocking his glasses off. They had a bayonet at his throat.

'Good afternoon, gentlemen,' he greeted them through a mouthful of broken teeth.

They dragged F3 down the marble steps. They took him across the road. The man with the Charlie Chaplin moustache appeared– red in the face – screaming.

Flint did not like dreaming about the next bit, and that might have been why he woke up. It was evening; twilight permeated the portholes, illuminating the chamber with a dim light. Sharp was softly snoring, but something was wrong.

The snatch squad had disappeared – and so had Alfie!

*

'They're in the Red Lion!' cried a voice from the trench phone. Flint guessed it was one of the Shepton Patrol's Secret Sweeties.

'The fools!' Sharp snarled. He glared at Flint as if it was his fault.

At least it was dusk – the time of day local bandits woke up and went looking for trouble. Sharp led Flint through the fields towards the nearest village – the one with the pub. 'Special Boat Section,' he muttered bitterly. 'I knew they'd be trouble!'

'I think they've lost their officer,' explained Flint. 'I think he was one of the casualties.'

'Special Forces officers are even worse than the rest of them,' replied Sharp. 'They're specially selected for being maniacs. None of them care much if they live or die, and they crave excitement.'

'Oh,' gulped Flint. 'Now, who does that remind me of?'

'I'm not saying they're not useful,' the bandit was saying. 'In fact, we couldn't do without them. It's just that . . .'

'They don't last very long?'

'No,' sighed Sharp, 'and nor does anyone who gets mixed up with them.'

They crept into the village in true bandit style, sneaking in from the fields until they stood like two shadows in the Red Lion beer garden. 'What those fools don't realise,' whispered Sharp, 'is that there are informers all over the place.'

'Informers?'

'People who tip off the Germans – sell information for money. British commandos have just ambled into a public house in occupied territory. Everyone in the bar will be slapping them on the back and wishing them luck – but it only takes one traitor to make a secret phone call, and the Waffen-SS will be thundering into this village with all guns blazing. Do you know how to use one of these?' Sharp adjusted his Sten gun and handed it to Flint. 'It's cocked and ready to fire,' he said. 'For God's sake don't drop it or it'll take your legs off.' He pushed the boy behind a wall. 'Cover the road,' he instructed. 'They're most likely to come from that direction.' He pointed right. 'They'll be in Henschel 33s – do you know what they look like?'

'Yes.' Flint's voice was just a little tense. Flint himself was just a little agitated. It wasn't just that he was afraid of dying – he didn't much like the thought of killing either.

'Aim at the driver. Don't wait until you can see the whites of his eyes – as soon as they come round the corner give it to them. Got that?'

'Yes.'

Flint heard Sharp's boots as they ran towards the back door. He could hear laughter and a piano. Snatches of song drifted across the beer garden from the crowded bar. 'On Mother Kelly's doorstep,' they were singing, 'down Paradise Row . . .'

The music suddenly stopped. Angry voices yelled. Sharp was telling the snatch squad exactly what he thought of them, and the commandos were answering back. *I wonder what Alfie's doing,* thought Flint. Headlights! A truck came bucketing round the corner – a single Henschel 33.

Caught in the beam of the headlights Flint could not see the driver. He aimed blindly at the speeding truck and squeezed the trigger. The gun kicked against his shoulder – a stream of lead shot towards the stars. *I've got to stop them!* Flint was desperate. He frantically lowered his aim until he was firing into the truck's windscreen. It swerved – struck a cottage in a shower of sparks – bounced back into the road and raced towards the Red Lion. The back of the truck was full of soldiers. They'd seen the gun; they knew where the lone marksman was crouching. Bullets ricocheted off the wall. Bullets sang past Flint's ears. He dropped under cover – out of range and out of sight. He waited, eyes wide in terror, pulse racing.

The truck squealed to a standstill. Boots hit the road. *They're coming for me!* Flint realised, but he did not dare look. There was a sudden chatter of submachine guns. Someone was racing down the beer garden.

'Shoot!' yelled Alfie. 'Don't just squat there!'

A grenade sailed over the wall and landed with a dull thump beside him. *This is it!* thought Flint. He was thinking very clearly.

He knew he was about to die.

Alfie pounced on the grenade and hurled it back over the wall. He dived to the ground, pulling Flint down beside him. There was an explosion; shrapnel whistled overhead. The Sten was wrenched from Flint's hands, and Alfie hurled himself into the fight.

'They've got no cover!' he yelled excitedly. He was firing into the road. Flint wondered which side he was talking about.

The gunfire stopped abruptly. Sharp appeared in the beer garden and took back his weapon. 'The snatch squad are another man down,' he informed them bitterly. It was as if he wanted to add, *And it serves them right!*

'Well?' asked Dr Six.

He removed his glasses, polished them with a silk handkerchief and replaced them on his button nose. He was in one of the state rooms in Windsor Castle – the one that was being used as an operational headquarters for the team searching for the abducted king.

'About an hour ago,' a female auxiliary informed him 'A truck load of infantry – a dozen men with an NCO – was ambushed in the Somerset village of Norton St Philip. All our men were killed. There appears to have been only one enemy casualty.'

'So what? Happens all the time!'

'Yes, sir,' replied the auxiliary, 'but an informer has been in touch with us about the incident.'

'And?'

'In the first place, Special Forces appear to have been involved.'

'The snatch squad?'

The female auxiliary nodded. 'We're almost certain

they were Special Boat Section,' she informed him grimly.

'Was there any sign of the king?'

'No, sir.'

'They'll have killed him,' muttered Dr Six, 'but at least the snatch squad has been sighted.'

'We'll hunt them down, sir!'

19

'**W**alk?' growled one of the three surviving snatchers. 'You want us to walk?' He shook his head at Sharp and stepped into the road to flag down a passing bus. 'Right,' he told the passengers, 'here's where you get out!' He waved his Tommy gun at the startled conductress. 'You too, Blossom,' he told her. 'As for you, my good man,' he turned to the driver, 'you are about to join the Resistance!'

'Am I heck!' was the emphatic reply.

'Queen and country, squire!'

'Don't you "queen and country" me, sunshine. I'm not going to get my head shot off just to please you.' So saying, the cautious driver opened his door and jumped into the night. Alfie clambered through the open door and settled himself down at the wheel.

'All aboard!' he yelled.

'I'm supposed to hand you over to a bandit from Yeo Patrol,' Sharp protested. 'You're supposed to be keeping to open country, not racing down the road in a bus!'

'Don't you worry about us, old son,' grinned the one with the hole in his ear. 'Alfie will drive very carefully.'

They saluted. They shook hands. They bid a fond farewell. 'Cheer up, Worzel,' they sniggered. 'You've got shot of us at last. You can plod back to your rat hole and report to Newfoundland. Tell them everything's going to plan!'

The snatch squad sped through the starlight with Alfie at the wheel. 'Tell us one of your jokes, Flinty!' he yelled. The commandos perked up; they turned expectantly in Flint's direction.

'I . . . I'm facing north,' he started nervously. 'That's the north star!' He pointed out of the back window. 'On my right hand is the east.' He pointed at a herd of cows. 'What's on my left hand?' He pointed at a flock of sheep.

The three ruffians looked baffled. They took a few swigs from the bottles they'd liberated and shook their heads.

'Fingers!'

A roar of approval greeted this appalling joke. The snatch squad was easy to please – they were like Doc Bolt in that respect.

'How do monkeys toast bread?' continued the young comedian. He skilfully raised his right eyebrow without so much as twitching the left. 'They stick it under the gorilla!'

No one groaned – they even hooted with hysterical laugher. It was Alfie who saw the headlights, in his offside mirror. Something big was following them – something big and military and certainly stuffed with soldiers.

The stolen bus was powered by gas; it had a huge, balloon-style bag on the roof. Gas-powered buses were fine downhill; it was going uphill they found difficult. Soon the chasing truck was less than two hundred yards away. The commandos smashed the back window and fired a few long shots.

'If they return fire,' cried Alfie, 'and hit our gas bag, we'll be blown into the next county!'

'What if we jump out?' cried Flint, whose wits had been sharpened by the jokes. 'If we wait until we go over the brow of this hill and jump out so the bus goes on downhill without us – then we could shoot at the gas bag ourselves. The Huns would think they'd hit it and blown us up.'

And that's exactly what they did. Alfie topped the rise and knocked the gear lever into neutral. The bus slowed to walking pace as it reached the top of the rise and started to roll downhill; it was easy to jump out. Flint landed with a clatter, the spool of film rattling under his shirt, and darted for cover while a quick burst of automatic fire blew the bus off the surface of the planet in a ball of flame.

'Sheeze!' whispered Alfie, digging Flint in the ribs. 'You're a genius!'

'For queen and country,' croaked the snatcher with the interesting ear.

'You're a pack of thieves!' growled the farmer.

Flint winced. Morning had broken. The cock had crowed, and an unsuspecting apple-cheeked farmer had clambered out of his bed, pulled on his trousers, clattered downstairs, thrown open the back door and sauntered into his farmyard only to find an eager team of ruffians helping themselves to his best tractor.

'We are within our rights,' said Alfie importantly. 'We can requisition whatever we need.'

'You'll be paid in full,' said Flint, 'when we win the war.'

'We're in a hurry!' snarled a snatcher. 'We can't stand about arguing all day or we'll miss the Pick-Up.'

The Pick-Up was important.

The sub would arrive off Honeysuckle Cove at the agreed time on the agreed date, and if the snatchers were waiting on the beach they'd be whisked across the rolling Atlantic to Newfoundland. The commandos didn't want to miss the boat, so soon the three surviving heroes – securely hidden under a load of hay – were driven away by two grinning boys on their requisitioned tractor.

'Shouldn't we keep to the fields?' suggested Flint. He was sitting on the mudguard – Old Kent-style –

wondering if now was the time he might learn to drive.

'Don't be daft! It would take ages driving from field to field. And we'd probably just go round and round in a great circle. We'll be OK on the lanes – just two farm boys and a load of hay.'

The tractor rounded a corner and collided with Vogler's new Mercedes.

The Gestapo man thought he recognised the boy at the wheel of the tractor, but could not pin the memory down. Not that it mattered. He was only a farm boy driving a little too fast. He looked at the other boy – the one wrapped in a coat several sizes too big for him. He couldn't see anything of his face apart from a pair of watching blue eyes peering at him from over the top of the coat collar.

If the three gallant snatchers had been alert, that would have been the last of poor old Vogler, but they were asleep and dead to the world. Even the collision had not disturbed them – not that it had been much of a crash, more of a jolt.

Flint was terrified. *Should I run round the back and tell them there's a Gestapo goon in the middle of the road? Best not,* he reasoned cautiously. *He's got an armed guard and Alfie would be smack in the crossfire.*

'Heil Hitler!' cried Alfie, raising his arm enthusiastically. *'Sieg Heil!'* He leapt out of his seat and jumped down to the road to inspect the damage. 'No harm done,' he told Vogler, 'just a bent bumper.'

The Gestapo man regarded the boy with a friendly smile. If he suspected mockery he didn't show it. Alfie was beaming affably.

'*Sprechen Sie Englisch, mein Herr?*'

'Yes, I do,' replied Vogler in perfect English. The boy did not seem to recognise him or to be surprised by the American accent. He was approaching the car.

'It would be quicker, sir, and easier, sir, if *your* driver was to reverse, sir. He's not towing a trailer of hay.'

How does he do it? Flint marvelled. *I'm sitting here huddled up in my coat looking guilty and suspicious, while Alfie's got them to back up out of our way. Now he's saluting and* Sieg Heil-*ing and waving his thanks.*

Alfie clambered back into the driver's seat and the tractor lurched forward as the Mercedes reversed cautiously towards a passing point.

'Bravo,' Alfie congratulated Flint, 'a masterly perform-ance!'

'What are you talking about?'

'Your village idiot impression – your two-bricks-short-of-a-load look – it's impressive! Little do they know they're face to face with the legendary son of the fabled Dingle Flint, or that the young daredevil has a spool of film under his shirt that will make Hitler gnash his teeth, spit blood and howl at the moon.'

'Shhh!'

'They can't hear us – all they can hear is this.' He revved the engine. 'Look at that cuddlesome Nazi smiling at you, Flinty – give him a wave!'

Flint sighed.

'Thank you, governor!' called Alfie as he drove past the parked Mercedes. 'Very nice car,' he addressed Vogler through the open window. He braked. 'If you don't mind me asking, sir, what model is it? My friend here thinks it's the W15 – don't you, Hercules?'

'Um,' gulped Flint.

'He's quite right!' replied Vogler with a cheery smile. 'But I'd be grateful if you could move your tractor.'

'Certainly, sir. I can see you're in a hurry. We'll be off, sir, with our load of hay. *Sieg Heil!*'

Twenty miles later the requisitioned tractor ran out of fuel, and Alfie cheerfully informed the commandos that they'd have to walk the rest of the way. They scrambled down from the wagon, brushing hay off their uniforms and complaining.

'It's not far,' Flint told them. 'We're nearly there.'

'Really?'

'I think so.'

The truth was that the boys were not familiar with the territory, and took a few wrong turns, which slowed the party down and set the snatch squad grumbling. 'What you boys fail to understand,' growled the one with the torn ear, 'is that a young lady is meeting me on Monday night at the Ship and Anchor, and the Ship and Anchor is on the other side of . . .'

'The pond?' asked Flint.

'That's right. If we miss the boat, that young lady will

be *very* disappointed. And so will I!' He wagged a finger under Flint's nose.

'And so will Lord Blade!' muttered Alfie. 'He's waiting for his spool of film. We're supposed to be at the beach at four,' he reminded them. 'Four in the morning – not four in the afternoon!'

'What will happen if we miss the sub?' asked Flint.

'You and Alfie will be held responsible,' grinned the one with the hole in his ear. 'You will be flayed alive and the pelts sent to Alberta!'

'Alberta?'

'Alberta – where they make the boots! And your guts,' he continued cheerfully, 'will be turned into garters, and presented to the queen.'

It was nearly dawn by the time they made it to Honey-suckle Cove. They came in from the road, the same way the doomed Secret Sweetie had been running the day she'd jumped the ditch into Three Corner Field. They were an hour late by the time they were on the beach, but a flash from out to sea alerted Alfie.

'There they are!' he cried. 'They waited for us!' He fished out his torch and returned the signal.

Flint gazed out to sea. He could hear the distant throb of the outboard, but could not make out the dinghy itself until it surged round Flat Rock and raced for the beach. He felt exhausted and relieved. What had Sharp said about Special Forces? – that they craved excitement and took crazy risks? – something like that. Well, what

Benedict Dingle Flint craved was a quiet life back on Honeysuckle Farm – and a full English breakfast. He'd be glad to see the back of them.

The spool! Flint reminded himself. He'd nearly forgotten the spool with the king's speech on it! He thrust a hand into his shirt, gripped it firmly, and handed it to the snatcher with the ravaged ear. The commando grabbed the film and slapped Flint on the back.

'Mission accomplished!' he growled. 'Next stop the Ship and Anchor!'

Now they were shaking hands and congratulating each other. The snatchers were describing life aboard a submarine. 'It's like being locked up in a tin trunk,' explained the one with the teeth, 'with a team of farting bears.'

The dinghy ran up the beach and a teenage boy – who just had to be a midshipman – leapt out to hold it steady. Then they were gone.

Flint and Alfie trudged up the hill towards Honeysuckle Farm. That was when they saw the devastation.

The farm was a heap of ashes, the barns broken and burnt. Everywhere cows and pigs lay slaughtered and stinking, under a cloud of flies.

And where was Jock the Border Collie?

20

'Why shoot all the animals?' asked Alfie, glancing anxiously about. 'What's the point?'

Flint was in tears. He looked around and pointed to the far fields, where heifers and bullocks were grazing placidly. 'It's only the milking cows they shot,' he said.

'Because they were here,' guessed Alfie, 'along with the pigs.' He was thinking deeply, still trying to work out what had happened and why. 'Anything that moved in the farmyard's been mowed down. The cows must have been here because it was milking time.'

'What about the Sweeties?'

'Maybe they were arrested.'

'Then they'd have been shot.'

'Only if the Germans knew they were SOE agents,' said Alfie hopefully. 'This doesn't look like a Gestapo job. It looks as if a unit of infantry turned up with orders to ruin the place.'

'The Sweeties might have been killed,' answered Flint with a catch in his voice. He'd been very fond of the two old bags. 'Their bodies might have been burnt when the Nazis set fire to the house. Shall we look for them?'

'What for?'

'So we can bury them.'

'If they've been burnt they won't need burying.' Alfie looked once more at the carnage, sniffed at the charred, acrid smell of the burnt house and the rotten stench from the farmyard, then thumped Flint's right shoulder urgently. 'Let's get out of here – we'll head for the Bolt Hole. Doc will know what happened.'

Flint nodded. The Bolt Hole had beds and food and friendship – he'd certainly like to be back there. But where he really wanted to go was the past. *I want to go back*, he thought sadly. *Back to before the invasion – I'd like to climb the apple tree – see Dad reading* The Times *and Mum swinging on the swing seat.*

With these thoughts of yesterday he ran to the pillbox, fished under the mattress, and stuffed one of his three books into a back pocket.

It was *William's Happy Days*.

They kept to the fields. The dead animals were close to

the road. Further afield, cattle and sheep were grazing contentedly as if nothing had happened. 'They must have just driven past shooting at anything in range,' muttered Alfie.

And that's when they found Turpin.

The huge horse was cropping the grass until he heard Flint's yell, when he trotted over. Flint stroked his soft nose. 'What happened? Where's Jock?' he asked the horse. 'Shall we take him with us?' he asked Alfie.

'Think about it,' muttered Alfie. 'What's he got here that he wouldn't have at the Bolt Hole?'

'Fields?'

'Fields, Flinty, fields – Turpin needs fields and a stream. That's what he's got right here, so leave the poor old fellow alone.'

'I suppose you're right.'

'I'm always right.'

'I'm glad you told me that, Alfie, because I'd never have guessed.'

'Would you not?'

'No – I'd have put you down as a one-boy disaster area looking for trouble in a state of constant confusion.'

'Constant confusion?'

'Constant confusion!'

It was early afternoon before they arrived at the smoking ruin of what had once been the Bolt Hole. A body lay outside the front door, riddled with bullets.

'They shot Ironside!' yelped Alfie, kneeling beside the

dead dog.

'Yes,' cried Flint. 'And who else?'

'We've seen no dead people,' said Alfie, 'just dead animals. They've been going round shooting livestock and burning down buildings. I expect they had a flame-thrower – same as they've used on the farms and ricks.'

'Why didn't the cellar blow up?'

'Don't know.' Alfie edged further away from the ruin just in case the store of Explosive 808 suddenly exploded. 'Maybe . . .' He was starting to say something important when he suddenly turned his head. 'Someone's coming!'

Flint could hear it too – the distant whine of an approaching vehicle. The boys scampered for cover, scrambled over a hedge, leapt across a ditch and sank out of sight behind a fallen tree.

The approaching engine wheezed, growled, and back-fired. From around a corner, the battered Trojan jolted and swayed until it rolled to a standstill in front of the slaughtered elkhound. The driver's door swung open and a grim figure in a boiler suit and a flat cap stepped out.

'Doc!' they yelled. 'Doc!'

'They've got Alice!' growled Doc Bolt fiercely. He was looking tired and tense. He'd not slept and he was sick with worry. But at least the boys had persuaded him to rest. He was cradled comfortably among the canisters of plastic explosive that they'd helped him excavate from the Bolt Hole cellar. Alfie was silently warming tins of baked beans in the smoking ruins.

'Where?' asked Flint anxiously. 'Where have they taken her?'

'They suddenly started burning farms,' Doc replied, 'for no particular reason that we could work out – all along the A35. We got all the trucks we could lay our hands on and went up ahead of them to warn people to get the hell out of the way. But then Aka suddenly decides to make a stand and ambush the convoy – troops, flame-thrower and all.'

'It had to be done,' said Alfie, fishing the hot cans out of the ashes. 'He had to attack. He couldn't just run away.'

'We lost some good blokes,' replied Doc, 'and we'd have lost a whole lot more if a commando squadron hadn't turned up.'

'A what?'

'Canadians – come over to wreck an air base. They saved our bacon, but we had to retreat . . .'

'You mean run!' muttered Alfie bitterly.

'Withdraw! We had to strategically withdraw, Alfie, leaving most of our trucks behind. Aka and the rest of the patrol are with the Canadians now – being ordered about by colonels and majors and saying, "Yes sir, no sir, three bags full, sir!" I was sent back for ammunition and explosives. I had to keep off the main roads, so it took hours – and this is what I found.'

'Where's Alice?' asked Flint again. 'Do you know where they took her?'

'No,' was the grim answer, 'not yet – but I'm going to find out, and you two are going to help me!'

Ten miles to the east, Dr Six stood on Black Bridge and looked down at the shunting yard beyond the sidings. It was full of displaced persons. He wrinkled his nose; displaced persons always smelt of damp sacks and urine. 'How many have you got here?' he asked Vogler, who was standing next to him leaning on his ebony-handled walking stick. His walrus moustache shone in the sunshine and shivered in the breeze.

'About a thousand.'

'How's the sewage system coping?'

'What sewage system?' chuckled Vogler. He did not approve of Dr Six. He thought his plan to ravage bandit country from sea to sea was mad. Farms had been burnt, cattle slaughtered, and now the civilian population was being deported. But he smiled a gentle smile. If he thought the little fellow in the thick pebble glasses was crazy, he certainly wasn't going to say so. If he thought it might – just possibly – be better for the Fatherland that Dr Six met with an accident, then he was not going to mention it.

It would come as a complete surprise.

Dr Six's eyes narrowed behind the famous glasses. 'Resistance fighters do not live in a vacuum,' he murmured thoughtfully. 'They live among the people.' He glanced at Vogler to see if he agreed. 'The people supply them with food and information,' he continued. 'This is what Operation Surprise Package is all about – isolating the bandits – destroying the farms that feed them and driving out all civilians.'

'I understand perfectly, dear Doctor. From now on anyone found in the forbidden zone may be assumed to be a bandit and shot. You have been very thorough.'

'It is necessary to be thorough when dealing with counter-insurgency measures,' replied Dr Six earnestly. 'Indeed, I'd be happier to shoot this lot rather than send them all north. It will be expensive to keep them all in camps, and there's always the danger of them escaping and finding their way back. But there'd be an international outcry. The Americans are already kicking up a fuss.'

'Let them bleat, my dear Doctor,' smiled Vogler. 'Let them wag their fingers and shake their fat heads!'

The makeshift holding camp was heavily guarded. Sentries stood at intervals along the railings that topped both sides on the embankment. Flint had squeezed himself through those railings on the dangerous night he'd started his apprenticeship, but now they were reinforced with barbed wire. Armed guards – one of them looking like a tortoise on stilts and another looking as if he'd like a glass of beer and a slice of apple strudel – were spread out at regular intervals, staring alertly into the crowded shunting yard for any signs of trouble. But the displaced persons were defeated, frightened and shocked. They sat in whispering huddles and waited.

Wolfgang could see a young girl sitting on a pile of railway sleepers quietly reading a book: none of these people would make trouble, he told himself.

There'd be no trouble at all.

Her Britannic Majesty Queen Elizabeth the Second popped a gobstopper into her mouth and sucked it thoughtfully. She was in Hut 23 – the one they'd converted into a cinema. The house lights were still on, and the place was empty apart from the teenage queen and her three Newfoundland dogs. She wasn't allowed ladies-in-waiting so she had dogs-in-waiting instead – and that was fine. In fact, it was an improvement; Newfoundland dogs didn't fuss.

The door opened and Lord Blade glided into the auditorium with one of his long, thin smiles. *Perhaps his lips are made from elastic,* thought the girl. *Perhaps they're worked by pulling a string. Maybe when he smiles he pulls a string, and if he pulled too hard the lips would meet round the back.* 'That would be very dangerous,' she whispered to Wellington. (Wellington was one of the Newfoundland dogs.) 'The top of his head would fall off – then where would we be?'

Lord Blade glanced up towards the little square windows behind which the projectionist was lurking and nodded. The lights dimmed. The curtains parted. Suddenly the young queen was looking at England – farms and woods, villages and church spires. Suddenly she felt homesick. A tear trickled down her cheek.

'We are somewhere in Occupied English Territory,' said a deep American voice. 'The rolling countryside looks the same as ever. But things are not the same.'

Wellington the Newfoundland gazed at the screen with keen interest; a team of fluffy bunnies was bouncing and flouncing in the corner of a meadow. He barked at them, but they took no notice.

'England's green and pleasant land is under the jackboot,' intoned the American gravely. Of all the deep voices for hire from the voiceover agency, his was by far the best. It dripped sincerity.

Wellington whined sadly; the fluffy bunnies had been left behind and a posse of armed ruffians was now stalking through the trees. 'The British Resistance fights on,' the voiceover was telling the world, 'and now this band of brothers has been joined by their former king.'

Elizabeth the Second practically choked on her gobstopper. There on the screen was the worried face of her wicked uncle! He was sitting uncomfortably on a tree stump and appeared to be wearing his dressing gown – or was it a smoking jacket? 'I was living in Portugal at the time of my brother's death,' he told the world. The young queen bit her lip and grabbed Wellington by his collar. *My father was executed!* she wanted to yell. *He didn't just die!*

Wellington sensed her mood and growled threateningly.

Lord Blade stood in the flickering shadows and watched the girl's tense face. She had shifted to the edge of her seat and was gazing raptly at the screen. He nodded his head. *She believes all this is real,* he chuckled inwardly, *and so will the Yanks!*

This was true. All over the United States newsreel

theatres were showing G106's little film, and Americans were saying, 'He's renounced the throne! He's living in the greenwood,' they said – the poetic ones who'd read Shakespeare. 'Like good old Robin Hood!'

It was at the Fox Newsreel Theater on Broadway that the film was watched by Korvettenkapitän Pfeiffer, the German naval attaché. He immediately contacted Berlin and informed Grand Admiral Dönitz – who told Heinrich Himmler, the Reichsführer of the SS. And Himmler told a tense, pale little fellow with a Charlie Chaplin moustache.

Who was not amused.

Alice found that reading about the Famous Five helped. She could bury her nose in the book and pretend everything was all right. All around her frightened people milled about waiting for whatever bad thing was going to happen next, but Alice felt as though she was safe in another world.

'You must be Alice Bolt,' said a friendly voice. The girl looked up, surprised; a tubby little lady was smiling up at her. 'I'm Flossie from Honeysuckle Farm,' she introduced herself. 'I know your friends Alfie and Benedict. Benedict's told me all about you and your Famous Five books.'

'Benedict Dingle Flint,' said Alice, putting a bookmark into *Five in Yellowstone Park*, which she was reading for the third time. 'He can burp at will.'

'Yes,' said Flossie. 'I've heard him.'

'He and Alfie are in the Resistance,' explained Alice from her perch on top of the sleepers. 'I'm surprised that the Resistance hasn't rescued us by now. Isn't that the sort of thing they do?'

'Well,' said Flossie, 'they're not supposed to engage the enemy head on if they're heavily outnumbered. They blow things up and shoot stragglers and assassinate people, but when the enemy turns up in force they melt away. Besides,' she said, 'they wouldn't be able to attack this camp without putting our lives at risk – and they wouldn't do that unless they thought the Nazis intended to shoot us – which they don't.'

'What I don't understand,' replied Alice with a frown, 'is why we've been here for practically a week.'

'It's because the Germans don't have enough wagons – suitable ones – to take away the people they've arrested all at once. This isn't the only holding camp. You've seen those trains going through – the ones with lots of big locked-up wagons with people yelling out of them? Well, those are the only ones they've got. They're using the same wagons every day – clearing out one camp after another and taking the people north to the camps they have on the moors. It won't be our turn until tomorrow.'

'Grandpa's still in bandit country,' remarked Alice thoughtfully. 'If he finds out they're going to send us away he's bound to do something about it.' She nodded her head decisively. 'He's brave and clever.' She nodded her head some more. 'And he loves me very much.'

Gosh, the Sweetie thought anxiously. *I hope he doesn't do anything daft!*

*

There was a charred, smoky smell in what was left of the Bolt Hole stable.

'We can do it!' That was Doc Bolt's assessment of the rescue situation. He popped a hunk of corned beef into his mouth and chewed thoughtfully. 'I remember back in the spring of 1918,' he told them. 'We were outnumbered three to one!'

'Did you still beat them?' asked Flint.

Doc frowned. 'Well,' he admitted, 'not quite.'

'We're not outnumbered three to one,' Alfie pointed out. 'It's more like twenty-three to one!'

'I'm not saying it will be easy,' Doc replied with a shake of his head, 'and I'm not saying it won't be danger-ous. All I'm saying is that it's possible – so long as we box clever. Very, very clever!'

Wolfgang was on the night shift. The dew had settled on his helmet and was dripping down the back of his neck. He stamped his feet. He yawned.

Wolfgang had his own private war aims, as you know. *Stay alive!* That was the policy. *Don't volunteer!* That was another. But the one he was thinking about as he stood in front of the reinforced railings was: *Get as much kip as you can*. When you were on guard you were not supposed to have a restful nap – if you were caught sleeping they might shoot you as a warning to the rest. At the very least you'd have a week or two in the cells being screamed at.

Wolfgang didn't like being screamed at, so this is what

he did: he unbuckled his belt and used it to secure himself to the railings. Then he leaned forward until the top of his helmet rested against a comfortable strand of barbed wire. No one would guess if he dropped off to sleep in that posture.

Unless he snored.

Maybe if I stuff a couple of fags up my nose they'd act as mutes, he mused, *like on a trumpet.* But he didn't stuff any fags up his nose; he just drifted off to dreamland with both nostrils snuffing happily at the night air – breathing it in – exhaling it out again – and, although he did snore very gently, nobody shot him. Sounds penetrated his helmet and his skull; they alerted his sleeping brain. But they did not wake him.

He heard footsteps – quick, light footsteps. They walked into his dream in the shape of an old man in slippers. An old man in slippers walked past in the dream, nodding pleasantly.

He heard Doc's wire cutters too – the quick, sharp clunk wormed its way into the dream as the sound of a tin of biscuits being dropped onto the floor. Wolfgang liked biscuits, especially butter whirls and ginger snaps; he often dreamt about them.

Wolfgang even felt the tip of a classic Fairbairn-Sykes fighting knife as it was pressed gently into his tunic adjacent to his left kidney. He was not stabbed, you understand. The knife was just resting at the right spot in case of unpleasantness.

It had been the sound of Flint's light footsteps that had

tiptoed into Wolfgang's dream, and it was Flint who was now crouching behind a pile of railway sleepers, waiting for daylight. The boy squatted by the sleepers and thought about all the things he had to do. He had a bag over his head, as you'd expect; a big brown bag with eye-holes was the nearest thing to a balaclava he could come up with. Wearing a bag over your head and keeping still is a good way to stay inconspicuous on a dark night, but once the sun peeps over the edge of the planet and the birds start singing you need to take it off.

Or you might draw attention to yourself.

The first person to see Flint squatting by the pile of timbers was Wolfgang. He recognised him at once as one of the boys on the barge. *What's he doing here?* he asked himself. *He wasn't here yesterday or the day before.* Wolfgang was puzzled. There was something about the boy that was suspicious – the worried, anxious way he kept looking about – and what was that he'd just pulled out of his pocket? Wolfgang squinted keenly through the railings; the boy was examining a knife. *The kid's armed!* Wolfgang realised. *He's just arrived and he's armed with what looks like a Fairbairn-Sykes fighting knife – the calling card of the British Resistance!*

A dim memory surfaced in his mind – the memory of light footsteps followed by a quick, sharp clunk. He stepped back to examine the barbed wire.

It had been cut!

It's that daft kid! said Wolfgang to himself. *What's he*

going to do – stab the train driver? He watched the boy put the knife back into his pocket. *I should report this,* he told himself. *Will the kid be shot or hanged? It'll be one or the other – after the Gestapo has finished with him . . . Best leave things as they are,* he reasoned at last. *They'd only ask how he cut the wire right beside me – and what real damage could he do – one kid with a knife?*

21

A train came rattling down the line and pulled up in the middle of the makeshift camp. The wagons had arrived, along with the platoon of Waffen-SS. First there was the engine – a Great Western Castle Class steam engine – then there was a single second-class railway carriage for the platoon. Next came the empty cattle wagons, ready for their human cargo.

Buffers, thought Flint.

He was madly thinking about all the things he was supposed to do – going over them again and again in his mind. This was the first time he'd ever been alone on a mission. Whenever he'd done stuff before (except in his daydreams) there had always been people ordering him about and telling him exactly what to do.

Hooks and chains, he reminded himself next. *Hooks and chains hold the wagons together – buffers lessen the shock when they jolt.*

'Benedict!' Alice suddenly emerged from behind her pile of sleepers. 'Have you come to rescue me?' The girl's dark eyes shone extra bright. Flint was so pleased and so relieved to see her, but he heard a faint, mumbling voice reply.

'Yes,' gulped this voice. It was coming out of his mouth, so it must have been his own. He listened attentively in case it said anything interesting. 'Yes,' Flint heard himself gulp. 'Not just you,' he heard himself continue. 'Everyone.'

'Everyone?'

'Yes.'

'All by yourself?'

'Um.' Flint's right hand was deep inside his right-hand pocket; he gripped his right hand round a wodge of what felt like plasticine and give it an apprehensive squeeze. Then he pulled his hand out of his pocket and sniffed his fingers. They smelt of marzipan.

'So,' Alice asked excitedly. 'What's your plan?'

'Er.' Flint wasn't exactly paying attention. His left hand was now deep inside his left pocket. It ignored Alfie's fighting knife snug in its sheath and gripped the timing pencil – the No 10 delay switch detonator.

Soldiers were jumping down from the second-class

182

railway carriage with fixed bayonets. They were yelling orders, rounding people up, herding them into the wagons.

'Don't get into the front one,' hissed Flint to Alice.

'What?'

'Get into one of the ones at the back!'

'But I want to be with you!'

'No,' whispered Flint. 'You mustn't! You want to be as far away from me as possible!'

From Black Bridge Vogler watched as the platoon gently encouraged the displaced persons into the wagons with the points of their bayonets. He smiled a happy smile. The news from Berlin was wonderful! Apparently Hitler had gone ballistic when he'd heard about the King-Emperor joining the Resistance. This was a disaster – a major blow. His masterly plan to legitimise the puppet government of the United Kingdom had been wrecked. And apparently he blamed Bat Ears.

What a shame!

The really amusing thing was that Dr Six was still wafting importantly about Occupied English Territory as if he was the Führer's blue-eyed boy. He still thought that because he'd once saved Hitler's life he was invulnerable.

The fool!

Dr Six came strutting along the bridge towards the smiling Vogler, his leather coat billowing behind him like the wings of a gliding fruit bat. His glasses gleamed pink in the early morning sun, while the blood-red ears stuck out jauntily.

'Good morning, Professor Doctor Six,' Vogler greeted him by raising his Tyrolean hat – the one with the feather. 'As you can see, the last thousand will soon be on their way.'

'Excellent, my dear Vogler, a smooth and effective operation. Let us hope we get credit for it in Berlin.'

'I'm sure we will, Doctor. Berlin keeps a close eye on Occupied English Territory.' Vogler smiled the ghost of a smile and turned to watch as the soldiers continued to herd the displaced persons. Both men leant over the wrought-iron balustrade as the engine whistled to hurry things up.

Five miles to the north Doc Bolt stepped back and examined his handiwork. 'Masterly,' he told Alfie.

'When was the last time you blew up a bridge?'

'It will be you that blows it up, not me. You're sure you understand exactly what to do?'

'Yeh.'

'If you make a mess of things at this end, Alfie, if you blow the bridge too soon or too late, we'll have a platoon of the Waffen-SS on our backs.' Doc glanced up and down the rail track. To his left was the dark mouth of a tunnel; to his right was a bridge over a river. He turned to Alfie and wagged a finger under his nose. 'Remember, *you* have to decide whether to blow it or not,' he reminded him. 'If Flinty fails to decouple the wagons from the carriage and the engine comes steaming out of the tunnel with the wagons still in tow . . .'

'I abort the mission.'

'You do. *Only* if that train comes racing out with *just* the carriage full of soldiers behind it do you blow the bridge – otherwise one thousand souls could plunge to their deaths.'

So that was the plan! What could possibly go wrong?

Blowing things up is quite easy if they've trained you properly and given you the right equipment, but ordering girls about can be difficult. A chap has to use honeyed words.

'I can help!' Alice was pleading. 'Please! Please! *Please* let me come with you!'

'No!' Flint heard himself gulp. 'You'd get in the way!' These were his honeyed words – but guess what? – they didn't quite hit the button. 'Anyway,' he continued quickly, 'it's too dangerous.'

In his dreams the legendary Firebrand Flint could coax and wheedle. In a case like this one he would have simply raised his right eyebrow, smiled a sardonic smile, and murmured softly, 'I say, old girl, but would you mind awfully if you went into Wagon 6? I know it's a frightful bore, but I need someone brave and utterly trustworthy in the sixth wagon just in case.' This is how the Firebrand would have dealt with Alice. But the real Flint was more the tongue-tied, gulping type.

It was the two Sweeties who came to the rescue. Flint was amazed to see them. He hugged them. He did not object when they kissed him.

'Alice must be in with you,' he told them urgently, 'in Wagon 6!'

The Sweeties understood at once. They helped push the girl into the wagon.

'Don't do it!' Flossie hissed at him. She'd guessed what Flint was up to; maybe she'd recognised the strong scent of marzipan.

But the boy was weaving through the milling mass of displaced persons, the only one amongst them who did not smell of damp sacks. He ducked and dodged through the throng, neatly avoiding the fixed bayonets, until he came abreast of Wagon 1 – the one that was coupled to the carriage in which the soldiers of the Waffen-SS would be travelling.

He understood what he had to do and why. He had to blow up the chain connecting Wagon 1 from the carriage full of soldiers. He had to do it when they were in the tunnel. That way the engine would pull the soldiers into the ambush, while the wagons full of prisoners would be safe. This is why it was so vital he got into Wagon 1.

He bent his knees and placed his hands on the edge of the wagon floor, ready to hoist himself inside.

'You can't come in here,' squawked a voice from within. 'We're choc-a-bloc, and it's Land Girls only.'

'You've got to let me in!' Flint half-squeaked, half-whispered. 'I . . . I'm Resistance!'

The ladies were not impressed – in fact, they giggled – but they let him in. A soldier slammed the doors shut, and, with a whistle, the train lurched forward.

It wasn't exactly dark in the wagon, because there were little narrow windows so the cattle wouldn't suffocate, but the space was jammed with giggling, teasing Land Girls, and that meant it was difficult to see what he was doing. The young bandit took out his screwdriver and started work.

Five miles down the line Alfie looked at his watch.

Meanwhile, the Land Girls were very interested in what Flint was doing and they provided a running commentary: 'He's taken up that floor board – with his screwdriver – and now he's looking through the hole.'

'Perhaps he needs a wee!'

Flint poked his head through the gap in the floorboards. The scents of smoke and steam met him out there along with the rattle of the wheels. Below he could see the coupling chain that attached them to the second-class carriage.

Good.

Sleeper after sleeper raced past in a blur. He stretched out a hand – clutched at a buffer – steadied himself and reached with his other hand for the almond-smelling wodge of Explosive 808. *Here goes! I must not drop it. That's right – squeeze it into the chain – wrap it round the middle link.* Gingerly he released his grip, anxious in case the wodge dropped away. *It's sticking! Now for the detonator.*

It was a standard SOE-issue pencil detonator with a timing mechanism. Doc had set Flint's for thirty seconds.

The boy pushed it gently into the plastic explosive and jabbed the switch. So far he was doing everything right. *Thirty seconds!* He pulled himself back through the gap in the floor – *One! Two! Three!* He looked at the floorboard he'd unscrewed. *Maybe I should drop it back over the gap*, he thought suddenly. *It'll act as a shield!* He grabbed at the board. He dropped it into the gap. *It'll shield us from the blast*, he told himself.

But Flint would have done better to have left the plank alone, because when the explosion came it hurled back the loose board and cracked it into his skull with the sickening sound of a hammer hitting a coconut.

22

The engine shot out of the tunnel with a whistle of steam.

Alfie gripped the flex. He was ready to connect it to the battery. He could see the carriage full of soldiers rolling along behind it. But there was no sign of the prisoner wagons; the train had been decoupled and they had been left behind.

Good old Flinty! He's done it! grinned Alfie as he gripped the flex tightly and made the connection.

The carriage soared thirty feet into the air. It rolled. It came twisting down. One end splashed and crashed into the river, while the other toppled on to the bank. The

Great Western Castle Class engine bounced off the rails, tumbled down the embankment, and landed on its side in a field in a fury of fire, smoke and steam.

Doc was running towards the crash. He had his Thompson submachine gun and glanced at the crashed carriage, ready to shoot any survivors. But no soldiers emerged from the wreckage. He ran down the line, towards the tunnel, where the prisoner wagons were rolling gently towards him. Doc raced from wagon to wagon unbolting the sides and heaving them open. When he reached the last one, Wagon 6, Alice leapt into his arms.

'Where's Benedict?' cried the Sweeties, jumping to the ground.

Doc had no idea, but something was happening at Wagon 1. A group of Land Girls had crowded round a body – the body of a boy.

'We closed his eyes,' a tearful Land Girl told the shocked and weeping Sweeties. 'They were wide open. It didn't look right.'

'We put his hands together,' said another. 'And Dolly's picking some buttercups.'

Alfie had to be pulled off the body. Alice had to be hugged by Flossie.

Doc was yelling at everyone. 'Leave him where he is! For Christ's sake get moving!'

Displaced persons poured out of the wagons. Doc marshalled them, yelling orders, growling at Alfie to pull himself together. Soon a ragged column was tramping across the fields, heading west towards safety.

It was at eight-twenty German Daylight Saving Time that Dr Franz Alfred Six saw the row of empty cattle wagons from the road.

'Stop!' he ordered his driver. He opened the door, stepped out of his Mercedes, put on his hat, and drew his revolver. 'Ring Major Vogler,' he told the driver. There was a radio telephone in the car. 'Tell him to get over here as soon as possible. Tell him what's happened.' Dr Six waved his revolver in the general direction of the silent wagons.

He had to climb up on to the line before he saw the wrecked engine or the soldiers' carriage. He stopped. He listened. He made his way cautiously down the other side of the embankment and examined the wreck of the engine. Both the driver and the fireman were dead.

Dr Six turned. Still gripping the revolver, he strutted towards the bank of the river. He stood motionless. 'Can anyone hear me?' he shouted.

There was no reply.

Dr Six climbed back on to the railway track. He stepped cautiously from sleeper to sleeper as he approached the first wagon. It had been unbolted, like the rest of them. Their sides swung open and Dr Six knew that they'd be empty. *Resistance!* he brooded grimly. *They'll be long gone by now.* He glanced at his watch then, as he came abreast on Wagon 1, he froze.

A pair of boots! A body!

Dr Six approached warily, ready to shoot.

There was a boy laid out. The eyelids had been closed, the hands placed together as if in prayer. A bunch of buttercups had been laid on his chest. Dr Six grabbed the child round the ankles and pulled the body towards him. He examined the passive face. Surely . . . yes, this was one of the boys who had been close to Windsor Castle when the King-Emperor disappeared.

He grabbed him under his shoulders and lifted him down to the track. *Still warm!* he noted as he dropped the child on to the chippings. *Head wound,* he observed. *It was obviously him that decoupled the wagons – killing himself in the process.* He searched the boy's pockets. *What's this? A Fairbairn fighting knife. Any papers – any identification? I don't expect so, but this looks interesting . . .*

Dr Six fished a bent and battered copy of *William's Happy Days* from a back pocket. He opened the cover and found what he was looking for – which was this:

If this book should dare to roam,
Box its ears and send it home

To:
Benedict Dingle Flint
Hornbeams,
Willow Way,
Shamley Green,
Nr Guildford,

Surrey,
England,
Europe,
The World,
Nr the Moon,
Nr Space,
Nr More Space

Dr Six squinted at the name and address. This was the son of Hitler's would-be assassin.

On impulse he crouched down and felt for a pulse on the boy's neck. Nothing. He pressed his fingers deep into the internal carotid artery. There was a faint flicker of life. *Dying, but not yet dead!*

'Doctor!' Vogler was approaching, limping with difficulty over the rough terrain. His moustache quivered, but otherwise he seemed unaffected by the scene.

'Resistance,' explained Dr Six. 'This boy is Benedict Dingle Flint – the boy you arrested at Honeysuckle Farm – the son of Dingle Flint, the assassin.' He held up the Fairbairn fighting knife as if further evidence was needed.

Vogler glanced to his left. They could not be seen from the road. He took the knife and held it for a moment, as if considering what to do with it. Then he drove it deep under the rib cage of Dr Franz Alfred Six, who collapsed to the ground with barely a sound.

'Killed in action,' he smiled, wiping the handle of the knife and placing it into the boy's limp hand. 'We'll just have to manage without him.'

He turned, gripping the ebony-handled walking stick, and began to limp back towards the road.

Flint could see himself lying on the chippings. 'That's me,' he said. 'I must be dead. Only I can think and talk to myself – so that's OK.'

He floated about for a while – which was restful – and wondered vaguely about Alfie and Doc. He was floating towards the tunnel – only it wasn't a railway tunnel any longer; it was a tunnel of light – it led him into a garden with an apple tree.

Benedict Dingle Flint stood under the apple tree and looked about the familiar garden. From out of the French windows strolled his dad.

'"And hast thou slain the Jabberwock?"' he asked with his jaunty smile. '"Come to my arms, my beamish boy . . ."'

23

Some of the older ones had not been able to keep up, but Doc Bolt would not wait for them. 'I'm old as well,' he growled. 'And if I run out of puff you must leave me behind too. The German army will be on our tail by now – we have to keep moving.'

So Alfie kept them moving. How he wished Aka and the Dart Patrol bandits were with them. How young he felt. And Doc looked so old.

They led the bedraggled line of the dispossessed across country. Doc insisted on them splashing up streams. 'In case of dogs,' he explained.

'Dogs?' cried Alfie. 'What dogs?'

'Bloodhounds,' Doc panted grimly.

Alfie glanced at him anxiously. The old fellow did seem to be running out of puff. Alfie fell back until he was walking next to Alice.

'We can't go on at this pace,' he whispered. 'Doc's exhausted.'

She shot him a frightened glance but said nothing. Alice had not spoken since she'd seen Flint's body. Her eyes were still bright with tears.

In the end it was a spotter plane droning overhead that stopped Doc's forced march. They sank down under cover. They'd made it to the wild woodland beyond the ruined Bolt Hole.

'Don't look up!' growled the old fellow. 'Don't move! We've done a good ten miles. Pass it on.'

'We've done ten miles!' called a Secret Sweetie.

'Ten miles!' echoed a farmer's wife.

'Ten miles!'

'We'll rest,' croaked Doc as the plane droned away.

If Dr Franz Alfred Six had still been in charge, the escaping party would have been rounded up by now – rounded up and shot. But Dr Six was no longer paying attention; he was lying on a slate slab looking surprised and stiff.

Very stiff.

Executing civilians was a waste, in Vogler's humble opinion – a waste of useful manpower and a waste of bullets. Besides, he'd been far too busy to bother about the rabble of escapees. First he'd had to limp back to the parked Mercedes looking shocked and upset. That had been OK; he could look sad when he had to. He'd dabbed his eyes with his Peter Rabbit hanky and spoken softly as if there'd been a lump in his throat.

'Knifed,' he'd gulped. The walrus moustache had quivered. The pale eyes had glistened. His voice had trembled. 'Assassinated!' He'd shaken his head – the Tyrolean-Alpine hat had moved sadly from side to side, and, from under it, Vogler's mournful voice had outlined the bloody details.

And then he'd driven to Gestapo headquarters in London.

The Westminster High-Security Zone was heavily guarded. There were checkpoints on the roads and at every tube station. Inquisitive squads of Waffen-SS patrolled the streets, stopping pretty girls and anyone who looked suspicious. The Gestapo had its headquarters in Kensington Palace, and it was there that Vogler arrived three hours and ten minutes after he had stabbed Dr Six with the Fairbairn fighting knife, wiped the handle and placed it into the limp right hand of Benedict Dingle Flint.

The palace was unscathed. It had survived the Blitz without bomb damage; it had survived the Battle of London without being shelled or burnt to the ground. In fact, it looked very much as it had done on the day Queen Victoria had been born there – apart from the odd bullet hole and the big Nazi flag.

As Vogler had hoped, Count Kasimir von dem

Wappenbuch had been appointed acting Gestapo Chief for Occupied English Territory. He was a man who commanded respect – a war hero, a flying ace from the Great War. Vogler limped into the orangery, where the count was seated comfortably in Dr Six's chair as he addressed the Death Squad chiefs.

'I do not mean to criticise the late Dr Six,' he told them with an amused sneer, 'but his methods were crude and his long-term strategy hopelessly limited.' The count ran a delicate finger over the scar on his left cheekbone and tapped his glass eye. 'It's coming up to two years since the invasion,' he observed with a sigh, 'and what exactly did the good doctor achieve in all that time?'

'He closed down the atomic weapons research base!' Stahlecker glared. He had been an admirer of Dr Six and did not like to hear him criticised.

'But we failed to capture any of their nuclear physicists or their secrets,' said Vogler. He seated himself at an empty chair, removing his hat and propping his walking stick against the highly polished conference table. 'They're all safe in North America, working on a very big BANG!' He shook his head.

'We've broken the spirit of the civilian population,' claimed Stahlecker. 'We interned all able-bodied adult males and dispatched them to Germany as industrial slaves! Surely that counts as a significant achievement!'

'Yes,' agreed the count wearily, 'but have we actually *secured* this island? Would you like your wives and children to join you here? Or might you think it just a little too dangerous for them? And what odds would you give that we'll still be here in two years' time?'

There was silence.

'Let us look long and hard at the conduct of this war,' hissed the count. 'If things go on in this way, the blood-crazed hordes of Muscovy will eventually be fighting their way through the streets of Berlin while the little teenage queen will be back in Buckingham Palace saying, "Off with their heads!" And it will be *our* heads that the young lady will be referring to!'

'What do you propose, Count?'

'Where is SOE based?'

'Newfoundland!'

'Then we must strike Newfoundland, gentlemen, before it is too late.' It was then that the count smiled one of his sardonic smiles. 'Dr Six may have been about as much use as a cat flap in a submarine,' he informed his chiefs, 'but we must still avenge his murder.' He turned to Vogler. 'Do you know who the assassin was?' he asked.

The Death Squad chiefs suspected that Count Kasimir von dem Wappenbuch himself had arranged the murder, but for some strange reason none of them raised these suspicions. Instead they shifted uneasily in their chairs.

'He was knifed under the ribs,' Vogler informed them sadly. 'When I arrived at the scene the poor fellow was writhing about coughing up blood. He recognised me, and although he was choking on his own blood he managed to speak. He was killed by a child.' The Death Squad chiefs gasped. 'A boy he identified as Benedict Dingle Flint.'

'The son of Dingle Flint?'

'No doubt of it. A boy's body, clutching what must have been the murder weapon, was lying by the side of the track. The good doctor must have managed to kill him while he was in his own death throes – although the boy had definitely not been shot, and Dr Six's pistol was still in its holster.' Vogler paused. He was feeding in the details – setting the scene to make it all believable. 'I made my way back to the road to summon help, but when my men arrived at the crime scene the boy had disappeared.'

There was an audible gasp from the assembled Gestapo chiefs.

The count half-guessed what had really happened. He knew Vogler shared his opinion that Dr Six had been a waste of valuable space, and he knew that the unassuming little fellow with the walrus moustache was clever and ruthless. But it was important for the world to believe that Dr Six had been murdered by the Resistance. There could be no doubt – no mystery – no rumours or whispers hinting he'd been knifed by his own side. Identifying a particular terrorist as his murderer, one with an infamous name, left no room for suspicion.

A young terrorist had been named as the killer. The count intended to make a big show of hunting him down. Lots of posters, a big reward on offer, house-to-house searches. If the boy was still alive he'd be hunted down – and shot like his dear old dad.

That would go down well in Berlin.

And that was why the very next day posters were displayed throughout Occupied English Territory:

**WANTED DEAD OR ALIVE
FOR THE MURDER OF
FRANZ ALFRED SIX**

BENEDICT DINGLE FLINT

£10,000 REWARD

24

Jock the Border Collie had been there when Honeysuckle Farm had been bombarded from the sea. He'd witnessed the mutilation by burning of Old Kent.

Jock knew that bad things happened.

This was why, as soon as the Germans hit Honeysuckle Farm, he'd run away. He'd heard the shooting. He's smelt the blood. He'd seen the smoke – but he had kept well clear. Jock had found Turpin, but he had not found the person he'd really been looking for.

He did not understand where Flint was; he knew that sometimes the boy was away from the farm for weeks on end, but had no idea where he went during these long absences. Jock had always lived at Honeysuckle Farm. For him the world was a very small place. Flint was bound to be somewhere in that small world; if he searched it he would find him.

For days Jock hunted for Flint. He went to every field that the boy had ever spread with dung; he went to Flat Rock; he roamed beyond the boundaries of Honeysuckle Farm into distant woods and further fields until, at last, he smelt a familiar scent.

The boy was lying on the chippings. His eyes were closed. First Jock licked Flint's pale face. Then he barked an urgent bark, before gently licking his ears. The eyes opened, first one and then the other. The boy mumbled something, then went to sleep again.

A truck full of soldiers arrived. Jock heard them yelling. He whined a warning. He growled. That did the trick.

The boy sat up.

Flint felt light-headed. He wanted rest – he longed to sleep again – he wanted to return to his dad's hug at Hornbeams, Willow Way. Maybe he'd go to bed in his old room. That would be nice – but Jock was growling again. Flint forced his eyes open.

Soldiers were approaching across the little strip of grass between the road and the rail track.

Flint lay still and watched as they ran up the embankment to marvel at the wrecked engine. He saw them rush out of sight towards the upturned carriage – this was his chance. He forced himself to his feet and, with Jock at his heels, staggered in the direction of the tunnel.

Flint made it into the shadows and dragged himself into the tunnel out of sight. He was truly back in Occupied English Territory now – back in the dangerous world. Hornbeams, Willow Way was just a memory.

'Alice and Alfie and Doc must think I'm dead,' said Flint. Jock thumped his tail against the chippings. 'If it wasn't for you I would be.' He gave the faithful hound a hug. There was nothing like a Border Collie for bringing things back to the fold. 'What's happened to them?' Flint wondered aloud. He knew that if the rescue was successful Doc's plan was to lead the displaced persons deep into bandit country – far to the west – away from the ravaged border lands. 'Maybe they were captured. Maybe they're dead. Perhaps they got away – what do you think, Jock?'

Jock had no idea.

It was three and a half long miles from the railway tunnel to Honeysuckle Farm. They did it in one short night.

The Type 28 anti-tank pillbox was very much as Flint had left it. His mattress was still in place. He climbed under his rugs and slept for a whole day. After that he slept for a whole night.

Honeysuckle Farm might have been wrecked and double-wrecked, but it still had chickens running about – and chickens laid eggs. Flint had eggs for his breakfast. For the best part of a whole week Flint ate eggs and drank water from the pump in the yard. And all the time he grew stronger – until the night he heard footsteps.

They were light, urgent footsteps. Someone was hurrying and scurrying past the ruined farmhouse. But Jock did not growl – he wagged his tail. He'd scented Taboo!

'Jock!' laughed a familiar voice. 'Where is everyone?'

'There's only me!' Flint called, struggling to his feet. 'Tumbleweed, is that you?'

'Benedict?'

'Yes!'

'I need your help and guidance,' she informed him breathlessly, 'so don't just stand there looking gormless.'

'It's pitch dark,' laughed Flint. 'How do you know I'm looking gormless?'

'It's intuition,' she explained merrily. 'I can tell. But you should be wreathed in smiles.'

'I *am* wreathed in smiles!' grinned Flint. 'I've never been so glad to see anyone in my whole life!'

'Come here, Benedict, and give me a hug. That's right! Golly, aren't you thin!'

This was good – being hugged by Tumbleweed in her soft woollen coat, sniffing her perfume, hearing her voice.

'Tell me all that's happened as you guide me alertly through the fields to my pick-up.'

'Pick-up?'

'Honeysuckle Cove,' she explained. 'It's become a sort of bus stop for submarines. Wasn't it fun!' she cried, squeezing his hand, 'snatching that ghastly little monarch! And that snatch squad – what a hoot! St John's

is absolutely hotching with people like that: you should
see George Street on a Saturday night – up to your knees
in broken glass, not to mention the odd severed head. But
they have the right spirit, Benedict, the up-and-at-'em
spirit. But where's Alfie?'

'I don't know.' He told her about the Bolt Hole, and
Alice, and the Sweeties, and the rescue, and how he
nearly died.

'Golly!' she gasped. And, 'Gosh!' she cried. 'I didn't
know anything about all this! I've been busy. But you
haven't said anything about Dr Six! Is it true?'

'Is what true?' asked Flint warily.

'What it says on the posters – didn't you know? You're
wanted dead or alive!'

'Wanted? Me?'

'Yes, my little hero! Dead or alive for killing Dr Six, the
foul and evil Dr Six, Chief Gestapo Goon for Occupied
English Territory! Don't tell me you don't know about the
posters – there's a huge reward. In fact, Benedict, now I
come to think about it, it is total and absolute madness
for you to be anywhere near Honeysuckle Farm. That'll
be the first place they'll look for you as soon as the penny
drops and they ask about farm boys answering to the
name of Benedict Dingle Flint – I'm amazed they haven't
swooped already! You say you have no idea where the
others are? That settles it – you're coming with me.'

'To St John's?'

'Of course to St John's. First we go to Iceland – you'll
like Iceland – so will Jock. Then we'll fly to Greenland –

you'll HATE Greenland. And finally we'll end up in Newfoundland – you'll LOVE Newfoundland! You can join HAVOC.'

'HAVOC?'

'They're an elite squad of teenaged commandos,' explained Tumbleweed, 'and they're an absolute hoot. You'll blend right in.'

'But what about Jock?' asked Flint.

Tumbleweed shrugged. 'He can come too.'

The boy sighed. This was hard. Abandoning England? Leaving all his friends behind? He hoped Alfie, Doc and Alice were all right, wherever they were.

'OK,' he said at last, his voice soft. 'Newfoundland. That's where my mum is.'

Remember me, she'd screamed the day they'd taken her away. And Flint had remembered.

He'd remembered every day.

'Do you have anything to pack?' asked Tumbleweed.

Flint shook his head. 'Only my books,' he said. There were only two of them left: *Right Ho, Jeeves* and *Biggles Flies North*. He stuffed them into his pockets and led the way through the dark to Honeysuckle Cove.

At exactly 0100 hours GMT HMS *Leopard* surfaced silently out in the bay. Hats appeared in the conning tower. Men in duffle coats gazed intently towards the land, to where the moving waters broke and sighed on Occupied English Territory. Flint could see the captain checking his watch and peering through his field glasses.

Soon a rubber dinghy surged up the shingle and a boy of about fourteen – he must have been a midshipman – leapt out to hold the bow steady and help Tumbleweed climb aboard. Jock jumped in after her, and Flint took his place beside them.

The midshipman pushed off and grabbed the tiller. He gave Flint a scornful glance. 'Off to St John's, are we?'

'Yes . . . I'm going to join HAVOC.'

'HAVOC?' The older boy laughed. 'They'll eat you for breakfast!'

Flint ignored him. He stroked Jock's ears. 'I might look like a startled canary,' he replied eventually, 'but I'm a bandit. I'm wanted dead or alive. Why would HAVOC worry me?'

Why would anything?

TIMELINE

(fictional events in italics)

1939

1 September – Nazis invade Poland

3 September – Britain, France, Australia and New Zealand declare war on Germany

5 September – United States declares its neutrality

10 September – Canada declares war on Germany

1940

9 April – Nazis invade Denmark and Norway

10 May – Nazis invade France, Belgium, Luxembourg, and the Netherlands

Winston Churchill becomes British Prime Minister

10 to 26 May – Battle of France – *300,000 British troops killed or captured*

12 May – Churchill appoints Max Blade (Lord Blade) Minister for Special Operations

14 June – Germans enter Paris

10 July – Battle of Britain begins

12 October – Operation Sea Lion (the invasion of Britain) begins

23 October to 1 November – Battle of London

24 October – Lord Blade takes Princess Elizabeth first to Scotland and then to Newfoundland

30 October – death of Churchill

5 November – Amos Q. Pearmouth elected President of the United States

1 November to 3 December – Occupation of England, Wales, and Scottish Lowlands

17 December – Failed attempt to assassinate Hitler at Trafalgar Square

1941

4 January to 16 February – Occupation of the Scottish Highlands, Northern Ireland, and the Irish Free State

ACKNOWLEDGEMENTS

The opening line of this book came out of nowhere: *They'd shot his dad, then they'd come for his mother*. The first person to see it was Claire at Rogers, Coleridge & White. She showed it to Catherine. 'That's great,' they said, 'but what happens next?'

That's what you need – people who say 'THAT'S GREAT!' And if they also tell you when your jokes fall flat or what you've just written is difficult to understand or boring or a total red herring or that Tumbleweed had *dark* eyes on page 23 and *blue* eyes on page 97, then that helps.

The helpful ones on *Never Say Die* were: Catherine Pellegrino; Polly Nolan; Rachel Leyshon; Laura Myers; and Barry Cunningham.

David Tinkler
Devon
April 2014

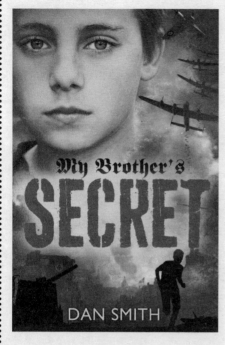